"I thin[...]

The assas[...]
opportuni[...]
camera, se[...] [...]
his adversary, and he staggered backward.

Bolan charged forward, intending to tackle him and take him down, but the man spun aside as he brought his fist down on the back of Bolan's head, driving him to the ground, stunned.

The assassin bent and flipped Bolan over onto the tracks, staring into his face. "You will never find us. You will never stop us." Then he took off again, racing toward an oncoming train.

Bolan tried to push himself up, tried to crawl to the narrow space next to the tracks, but his body refused to obey his commands. The train's headlight was blinding, the thunder of its approach drowning out everything.

The Executioner's last thought before blackness took him was that this was not how he'd expected to die…

MACK BOLAN ®
The Executioner

THE EXECUTIONER

DON PENDLETON'S

COMBAT MACHINES

A GOLD EAGLE BOOK FROM

W☉RLDWIDE®

TORONTO • NEW YORK • LONDON
AMSTERDAM • PARIS • SYDNEY • HAMBURG
STOCKHOLM • ATHENS • TOKYO • MILAN
MADRID • WARSAW • BUDAPEST • AUCKLAND

First edition December 2016

ISBN-13: 978-0-373-64449-0

Special thanks and acknowledgment are given to
Trevor Morgan for his contribution to this work.

Combat Machines

Recycling programs
for this product may
not exist in your area.

Printed in U.S.A.

Obedience to lawful authority is the foundation of manly character.
—Robert E. Lee

Human beings often need an ideology to give their lives meaning and purpose. But unquestioning obedience to any doctrine is just as dangerous as having none at all. It can lead to terrible crimes committed in the name of these beliefs. And when that happens, that sort of ideology must be stopped—by whatever means necessary.
—Mack Bolan

THE
MACK BOLAN
LEGEND

Nothing less than a war could have fashioned the destiny of the man called Mack Bolan. Bolan earned the Executioner title in the jungle hell of Vietnam.

But this soldier also wore another name—Sergeant Mercy. He was so tagged because of the compassion he showed to wounded comrades-in-arms and Vietnamese civilians.

Mack Bolan's second tour of duty ended prematurely when he was given emergency leave to return home and bury his family, victims of the Mob. Then he declared a one-man war against the Mafia.

He confronted the Families head-on from coast to coast, and soon a hope of victory began to appear. But Bolan had broken society's every rule. That same society started gunning for this elusive warrior—to no avail.

So Bolan was offered amnesty to work within the system against terrorism. This time, as an employee of Uncle Sam, Bolan became Colonel John Phoenix. With a command center at Stony Man Farm in Virginia, he and his new allies—Able Team and Phoenix Force—waged relentless war on a new adversary: the KGB.

But when his one true love, April Rose, died at the hands of the Soviet terror machine, Bolan severed all ties with Establishment authority.

Now, after a lengthy lone-wolf struggle and much soul-searching, the Executioner has agreed to enter an "arm's-length" alliance with his government once more, reserving the right to pursue personal missions in his Everlasting War.

Prologue

Mostar, Herzegovina
July 6, 1992

The distant, steady whistle and *crumpf* of artillery shells landing in the city scarcely bothered Andreja Tomić anymore. When the siege had first begun three months ago, she'd spent many exhausted, sleepless nights waiting for the next shell to land on the building she was living in. Now, however, the barrage's constant din and its incipient danger had been relegated to the back of her mind, acknowledged, but not dwelled on. Not when she had so much work to do. Now, she was mostly just exhausted.

Mostar had been the scene of a pitched battle for control of the city and the surrounding area since that spring. The Yugoslav People's Army, or JNA, had invaded in early April and seized control of a large portion of the city. A sustained counteroffensive by the Croatian Defense Council, or HVO, had pushed the JNA forces out of the town, but they had retaliated with their ongoing artillery barrage, which the HVO was replying to in kind.

At first, Andreja had feared for those under her care, but the JNA had seemed to be directing their fire on more valuable targets, at least in their minds. She had her doubts about that. In the past few weeks, the seemingly endless rain of munitions had claimed a Franciscan monastery, the Catholic cathedral and bishop's palace. The destruction wasn't all carried out by the JNA. After retaking the city, the HVO had demolished the Serbian Orthodox Monastery, as well as the Orthodox Cathedral Church that dated back to the mid-nineteenth century.

But the Kriva Cuprija, the Sloping Bridge, one of Mostar's oldest man-made landmarks, still stood, spanning the Neretva River as it had for the past four hundred years. Every morning, when Andreja awoke, she looked out through the smoke and dust of the previous night's bombardment to see if the white stone arch still stood, and every day when she saw it, she breathed a little easier. In a way, the old bridge was a symbol of the town—as long as it stood, then so would Mostar.

When she was little, Andreja's grandmother, Marica, had told her stories of the destruction that had ravaged their nation during World War II, when the Ustaše, the Croatian Revolutionary Movement, had carried out a genocidal war against the Serbian population as well as Jews and the Romani in their attempt to create a "pure" Croat nation. Andreja remembered the nightmares she'd had from hearing those stories, and the fierce arguments between her grandmother and her mother. The older woman had stated that the next generations had to be prepared for the violence that was sure to return, while Andreja's mother had shaken her head and dismissed her own mother's claims, preferring to look ahead instead of back to the past.

As a child, Andreja hadn't believed her grandmother. Now, however, she found it hard to remember any peaceful time. If the devastation inflicted on the city was anything close to what her grandmother had endured, Andreja didn't know how anyone had survived it.

Now she was enduring it, as well. The worst parts were the intermittent utilities and constant food worries. With the city cut off from foreign aid and supply convoys, electricity, working sewer systems, food and water were in short supply. So far, they had been hanging on, but with the siege showing little sign of ending anytime soon, Andreja dreaded the day they would eventually run out, and she would have to begin making the next series of hard choices in a life that had already been filled with so many.

But for now, she had to begin taking care of her charges, and do whatever she could to see them through a new day.

She used a scant half liter of her allotted water ration to wash her face and hands, and had to be content with that for now—a bath or even a brief shower was a luxury she could not afford. She dressed in her uniform of a dove-gray, ankle-length dress with a yellowed apron over that, and twisted her long hair into a tight bun and tucked it under her white cap. Then she left her small house on the hill and walked down the path toward the main building, keeping her head down and her shoulders hunched over in anticipation of an errant shell landing nearby. When she reached the corner of the building with no harm done, she relaxed a bit and looked up—only for her mouth to fall open in shock.

A truck was parked in the driveway, a relatively new

one, with a driver sitting behind the wheel. She didn't know to whom it belonged, or what its occupants were doing here, but she intended to find out.

She entered the building's foyer to find her two assistants anxiously awaiting her. Luka and Nenad were barely out of their teens, and had been pressed into service here when their families had been either captured or killed in the fighting. Andreja had taken them in and trained them to handle some of the crushing workload she had been managing alone until then.

Upon seeing her, the two young women hurried over. "Thank goodness you are here, Andreja!" Luka said, her words echoing around the bare room.

"Keep your voice down!" Nenad scolded. "You'll wake them!"

"All right, calm down, both of you," Andreja said, raising her hands for peace. "Who are our visitors? We have no one scheduled until the end of the week." That was when, supposedly, more supplies were supposed to arrive from the HVO. They made it through about 50 percent of the time.

"He said his name is Dr. Rostislav Utkin, and that he is a scientist from the Soviet Union," Luka said.

"You mean Russia," Andreja replied. Although the USSR had broken apart almost three years ago, old habits died hard in the areas surrounding the former empire.

"Yes, she does," Nenad said with an exasperated huff. "He said he wishes to inspect the children."

Andreja's dark brown eyes narrowed at that. "To what end? Are you saying that he wishes to adopt?"

Luka threw up her hands in confusion. "All he said was that he wished to inspect the children, and that he would wait for your arrival."

Andreja glanced at her closed office door. "Well,

then, let me go in and meet this Dr. Utkin, and find out what he has to say for himself. You two go and make the children as ready as you can. If all seems in order, we will join you shortly."

The two young women nodded and crossed to a pair of large double doors on the other side of the room. Opening them just wide enough to slip through, they disappeared into the room beyond.

Taking a deep breath, Andreja squared her shoulders as she strode to her office door and opened it.

The room on the other side was small, just large enough for her compact desk, wheeled, creaky office chair, and two others in front of the desk. A dusty, battered file cabinet sat in one corner, its top drawer open. A man sat in one of the chairs in front of the desk, reading a file.

"What do you think you are doing?" she asked as she swept around the desk and snatched the limp manila folder from his hand. "These files are private. You have no right to read them."

The seated man regarded her from behind wire-rimmed glasses. His light blue eyes appraised her, taking in everything from her simple dress to her drawn, pale face and the shadows under her eyes.

He spread his hands in a vaguely penitent manner. "Please excuse my intrusion," he said in passable Bosnian. "I did not know how long I would have to wait, and well, I am afraid that my eagerness got the better of me." He smiled, his thin, bloodless lips curving up and somehow softening the otherwise severe planes of his face. His white-blond hair was cut short enough that she could see his scalp through it.

"That is no excuse for barging in here and looking through whatever you wish." She put the folder back in the cabinet and pushed the drawer closed, then walked around to stand behind her desk. "Now, why are you here, Dr. Utkin?"

"Straight to the point. I like that." He leaned forward, his eyes gleaming. "Why, to adopt some children, of course."

Andreja blinked. "Children?"

"Yes, I'm looking for at least twelve if possible, assuming they meet my criteria. Of course, this is not the only orphanage in the country, but given the growing troubles near Sarajevo and Zenica, I felt this one might be the best place to start."

"Why would you wish to adopt twelve children?" Andreja asked as she sat, alarm bells sounding in her mind.

Utkin peered at her for a moment, then nodded. "Ah, of course. You are thinking that because I am from Russia I am procuring children for some sort of medical experiments or something. It is nothing like that. The Ministry of Health has authorized a long-term program to raise children who otherwise might not have the opportunity to become productive members of society, and give them such advantages to become so, and study how they develop over the years."

Now Andreja frowned. "The Russian Ministry of Health wishes to adopt children from our country to raise in yours?"

Utkin spread his hands again. "That is pretty much the idea."

"But why *our* children? Surely your country has orphans of its own that need homes?"

A brief smile flitted across the doctor's thin lips. "Your concern for my people is touching. While it is true that there are parentless children in our country, they often have mitigating circumstances that already impact their early development for good or ill. For the purposes of this extended study, we wish to find infants with absolutely no previous attachments to people or places. Blank slates, if you will pardon the expression. They will be very well cared for and have everything they need provided. They will receive a first-rate education, access to the best health care and a structured environment that will, hopefully, allow them to grow up to reach their full potential."

"And you believe that you are taking these children from a negative situation and placing them into a more positive situation in your own country?"

He nodded. "Miss Tomić, I am aware of the circumstances under which the children in your facility were conceived. I know what kind of life they have to look forward to without intervention from somewhere—wards of the state, with mothers that reject them and unknown fathers. Shuttled from state facility to perhaps a foster home to another facility, never receiving the care and education they so desperately need—and which we are willing to provide." He leaned forward and smiled, the expression lighting up his severe expression. "You need help here. We are willing to help. Please…let us help you."

It was that last part that finally removed Andreja's resistance—the feeling that he truly cared about what would happen to these children. "Why don't we take a walk into the ward, and you can have a look at the babies?"

"I would like nothing more," he replied as he rose to his feet.

Andreja walked with him out of her office and across the foyer to the double doors. She gently pushed them open and peeked inside.

Luka and Nenad were busy among the more than three dozen cribs, efficiently changing diapers. The rustling of their clothes and of the cloth diapers was the only sound in the room. None of the infants made a sound.

Dr. Utkin nodded pleasantly to her assistants, then focused on the four rows of children, ranging in age from six to eighteen months. He began walking up and down the rows, leaning over to examine this child or that.

A shell arced overhead with a scream, then detonated close enough to rattle the windows. Even then, not a single baby uttered a sound.

"I have heard of this, *da*?" Utkin asked. "Since the children do not get comforted when they cry, they learn to not cry, as it does them no good."

"I'm afraid so," Andreja replied.

"It sounds cruel, but this actually works better for our program," Utkin said, clasping his hands behind his back as he walked. "We will be examining their ability to form relationships later on in life, after having those needs withheld as infants. It is said that the brain develops differently under such adverse conditions, and we will find out if that is so, and how it manifests later on…"

He turned to see the grim expression on Andreja's face and reached out to touch her shoulder. "Of course, I did not mean that you and these young ladies are responsible for their development. You are doing all that you can, of course."

"Yes…it is not easy," she replied. "We should continue your tour."

"Yes, of course." Utkin walked up and down every aisle, looking at each child. At length, he came to the end of his inspection. "Are there any more?"

"No, thank heaven."

"Very well. I have made my selections." Utkin began walking up and down the aisles again, stopping briefly at a dozen cribs, each one just long enough for Andreja to note which one it was before he moved on to the next. In just a few minutes, the tall, lean scientist had chosen more than a quarter of her current children.

"Very well. They can be ready for travel by this afternoon." Andreja cleared her throat. "I assume that you have brought the necessary supplies? We cannot spare anything to send with you."

Utkin nodded. "I understand. We brought all that is necessary for their safe and healthy journey back to Russia. After all, they represent a substantial investment on the part of the motherland. It would be terrible if something happened to them before they arrived in their new home."

"Well, while Luka and Nenad are preparing the children, you and I can head back to my office and begin the paperwork for all this. Twelve sets. I'm afraid you're going to be here awhile."

"That's quite all right," Utkin said with a smile. "I want to make sure everything goes smoothly for them from this point forward."

FOUR HOURS LATER, with the paperwork completed and the dozen babies safely loaded into infant seats secured inside the truck, Utkin extended his hand to Andreja, which she took.

"Thank you for your assistance. Given the circumstances, I'm so very pleased that it went as easily as it did."

"And thank you, Doctor. I certainly hope that you will be able to give them a better life. Although I would like to know how your experiment turns out, I will be content just knowing that they escaped this place."

The doctor nodded. "Yes, together we have saved twelve lives today. They and I owe you our thanks."

"No, it is you who has our thanks. They are the recipients of your generous offer, and I know they will do well by it."

Utkin nodded even as he checked his watch. "I'm afraid, however, that we must be going. It will be difficult enough moving through the checkpoints, and exiting the country with twelve infant children that I didn't have upon my arrival, we probably won't get out of the country for a week with all the paperwork that will have to be examined."

Andreja smiled and nodded. "Of course. Go with God, and safe travels."

"Thank you."

With that, the doctor climbed into the passenger seat of the truck as the driver started it up.

"Get what you came for?" the driver, Utkin's assistant and bodyguard, asked around a cigarette he lit.

Utkin glanced back over his cargo, the twelve children sitting silently in their car seats. Any trace of the kindly social scientist had disappeared the moment he'd gotten into the vehicle. Now he regarded the children coldly, dispassionately, as if they were rats in a cage.

"Oh, yes, Dimitri," he murmured. "They will do perfectly." He turned to face the front of the vehicle again. "You radioed in the coordinates, yes?"

The driver nodded. "As requested. In fact, they should be reducing that building to rubble right…about…now."

"Yes, with all records lost as a result of an unfortunate accident." Utkin grinned, a wolfish smile with no humor in it whatsoever. "You are very fortunate, Dimitri. Not many people get to witness history being made firsthand."

The other man grunted, jetting smoke out of his nose.

"Yes, for you see, the new vanguard of Russia's soldiers is beginning today." Utkin swept an arm back to encompass the dozen children. "And these will be the first of many."

1

Ground Forces of the Russian
Federation Headquarters
Moscow, Russia
The present

Dr. Rostislav Utkin walked into the main building of
the Russian army headquarters, presented his identification to the guards inside, submitted to the metal detector and physical search and checked in at the desk
behind the checkpoint.

He hadn't changed much in the past twenty-plus
years. He was still tall, but now slightly stooped. His
white-blond hair had receded from his forehead and
had thinned all over, to the point where he now wore it
cropped so close he might as well have been nearly bald.

He was also leaner than he had been two decades earlier. The stress of keeping the funding, equipment and
staff together for his project through the intervening
years had taken its toll, but it had all been worth it. Now,
he was at last going to present the results of his pro-

gram to Oleg Istrakov, the new colonel general. He was confident that when his superior saw the results of his program, he would renew his funding. Utkin hoped he might even authorize its expansion so they could begin locating and training the next generation of soldiers.

A lifetime of theories, of work and planning, favors bought and sold to keep his program running, all of it was about to pay off in the next few minutes.

Utkin took a seat outside the colonel general's office and sat patiently, not distracting himself with a smartphone or newspaper, instead running over talking points, attempting to anticipate questions and objections, and rehearsing the best ways to either answer or counter them.

Istrakov's schedule had to have been running smoothly, for the door opened after less than ten minutes and a black-haired, suited man stalked out, his expression glowering.

Utkin recognized Professor Sergei Mentov, a mechanical engineer who had been tasked with developing the motherland's next generation of mechanized armor. The doctor didn't envy his job. Between the government graft and constant cycles of budget cuts, it would be a wonder if the good professor could field an armored tricycle within the next decade. Given his demeanor as he strode past Utkin without acknowledging his presence, even that seemed unlikely.

"Dr. Utkin, the colonel general will see you now," the secretary said from the doorway.

Utkin stood, checked himself over one last time to ensure he was presentable and walked into the small room adjacent to the man's office. With a polite nod to the secretary as she returned to her desk, he continued into the colonel general's domain.

The office was a reasonable size for the man's position, neither too big nor two small. Istrakov's desk was at the far side of the room, with two chairs facing it. A threadbare rug muffled Utkin's footfalls as he crossed to the desk and stood waiting to be recognized.

With a soft grunt, Istrakov finally looked up. He was a pale, bloodless man, his eyes slightly magnified behind rimless glasses. Utkin felt unease start to stir in his gut—the man looked like an accountant, not a former battlefield soldier.

Istrakov blinked owlishly, and his first words did not generate any more confidence. "You are my 2:15, yes?"

Utkin blinked. He knew the man was new to his position, but such an impersonal address threw him a bit. "Yes, Colonel General, Dr. Rostislav Utkin, at your service."

"Right. Please, sit." Istrakov waved at the chairs in front of the desk. Utkin did as instructed, sitting on the edge of his seat as the man tapped keys on his computer.

"Utkin, Utkin, Utkin…ah, here it is." Istrakov read something on the monitor, nodding as he did so. After a few moments, he looked at the doctor. "We are terminating your program. All funding will cease immediately, and you are to discontinue all current research, development and experiments."

Utkin just sat there and blinked for a moment, scarcely believing what he had just heard. "Sir, I was given to understand that this was a progress review, not a funding meeting—"

Istrakov shook his head. "I am sorry you feel that you were misinformed about the purpose of this meeting. The latest directives from the Kremlin are to review and evaluate all programs deemed unnecessary to the current goals of the Russian Federation. After careful consideration, your program has been determined to be costing an exponentially large amount in comparison to its overall utility."

Having gotten over the shock of the other man's announcement, Utkin quickly rallied. After all, this wasn't the first time his program had come within a hairbreadth of cancellation. "Sir, if I may, the units have only recently been brought on line in their full capacity. The field tests have been incredible, far exceeding even my wildest hopes. You cannot pull our funding now, not when we are ready to actually make the units available for real-world operations—"

"I can and will, Doctor. Such small-scale programs like yours, with such long gestational periods, are not what the Federation is looking to develop today." He glanced back at the screen and his light brown eyebrows rose. "Frankly, I'm amazed that you've managed to keep the lights on all these years—an impressive accomplishment in itself."

"Pardon my bluntness, but that is primarily because I kept your predecessors up to date about our progress, and to a person, they all agreed that my program was effective, worthwhile and, above all, necessary."

Of course, it was a lot easier to push through the bureaucracy when the oil money was flowing, Utkin thought.

"If you would just take a closer look at what we've been doing, or perhaps a demonstration of some of the units' various capabilities might convince you otherwise—"

"I admire your single-minded persistence, Doctor, but I have made up my mind." Utkin opened his mouth to continue his attempt, but Istrakov shook his head. "Are you aware of just how many programs I have to evaluate in the next two weeks? I have reviewed your summaries, and in many areas, I must admit that the results you have achieved are impressive. But the training and preoperational period is completely unacceptable for the results you are claiming."

"But we are now ready for true fieldwork, sir," Utkin persisted. "Just find my units a mission and let them execute it. Then you will see what all that money and time has purchased."

"At the moment, there is nothing that requires their specialized abilities. Your creations are not useful on the general battlefield, or training soldiers in Syria. They are highly specialized weapons, suitable only for things that we are not doing now."

During Istrakov's last comments, Utkin had run through several possible gambits in his head and evaluated the hazards of each. Like most good Russians working in the military and the government, he had a wide range of knowledge about things he probably shouldn't have known about. Bringing any of them up, even in a roundabout way, might simply get him a quick trip to the gulag.

But after another second's consideration, he decided to gamble on exposing a bit of what he knew—if he could just keep his program going another six months, it would be worth the risk. "Begging your pardon, I am aware of several initiatives that have been discussed at certain levels of our military that my units would seem tailor-made for. Particularly ones in the Far East, and in North America, as well."

Istrakov's brows narrowed. "Perhaps they would, but those various operations are all theoretical at best, and many are years from actual implementation. You are asking us to allocate millions of rubles a year to keep these units ready on the off chance that one of these programs *might* be enacted in the future. I'm afraid not, Doctor."

Istrakov stared dispassionately at him. "I have my orders to cut the budget wherever I can, and your program is on the chopping block. It is that simple. You have two weeks to make whatever preparations are necessary for reassigning your personnel—"

"And exactly how do you suggest that I do that?" Utkin asked, letting his overall anger finally seep into his tone. "As you said yourself, these are not merely frontline soldiers, or even special forces personnel. They cannot simply be 'reassigned.'"

"I understand. Your notes state that many of their internal systems can either be deactivated or removed. I suggest that you begin scheduling the necessary surgeries to make sure these units of yours will be able to function appropriately in their new assignments. Please be sure to follow proper procedures in doing so, including any letters of commendation or recommendation that would be required." Istrakov leaned back in his chair and folded his hands. "Do you have any other questions, Doctor?"

Utkin just sat there for a moment, blinking. Istrakov stared back at him until the silence grew oppressive. "Doctor, are you all right?"

With a start, Utkin shook himself and nodded. "Yes, sir, my apologies. This is all rather sudden. You had said I have two weeks to wind the program down, correct?"

"That is correct." Istrakov was already focusing on his monitor again. "Any further issues or questions that arise during that time can be sent directly to my office."

It was clear that the meeting was at an end. Utkin slowly rose and walked out of the office like a man in a trance. With a polite nod at the secretary, he left, walked down the hall past the entry checkpoint and out the door.

Blinking in the sudden weak sunshine, Utkin stood to the side of the headquarters entrance for a few moments, gathering his thoughts. Although a part of him had always known this day might eventually come, to be denied when they were so close to success was the bitterest pill to swallow.

Two weeks…two weeks to shut everything down, he thought while he walked down the broad avenue, oblivious to the other passersby.

He had gone a couple blocks when it struck him that perhaps he had been given two weeks to prove the efficacy of his program.

So, what if he were to show them what his program can do? The thought was so antithetical to his normal scientific mode of operation that it stopped him in his tracks. Several reasons came to mind—with his potential death factoring heavily in more than one—but he brushed them aside impatiently.

And once he removed any thought of personal survival versus what he hoped to gain—the continuance of his program—the reality of his situation was stark. Why not? He had nothing to lose anymore.

Overcome with the ramifications of the decision looming before him, Utkin looked around for somewhere to sit for a minute. He had wandered farther than expected while pondering his future, and now stood in an unfamiliar neighborhood of dingy shops interspersed with what looked like bars. Utkin frowned—he'd had no idea these places were so close to the military headquarters.

Selecting the nearest one, he stepped inside, wrin-

kling his nose at the overwhelming smell of stale cigarette smoke. He wasn't a puritan, just not fond of the odor.

Sitting at the bar, he ordered vodka, and when it
came, he reached for the shot glass and was about to
knock it back when he stopped and stared at the drink
in his hand, then set it back down.

No, he thought, if I am to do this, let it be my decision alone, unmodified by drink or anything else but my
own conviction. He would use the remaining program
funds for a series of missions.

Tossing some rubles on the bar, he left the full shot
glass and walked back outside, now a man on a mission.
Within another block, he found what he was looking
for—one of the new payphones that allowed a user to
access the internet, pay their utility bills, or even use
Skype to call people.

With a surreptitious scan of the area, he picked up
the receiver and dialed a number.

It rang twice before being picked up. *"Da?"*

"This is Father Time," he said. "The alarm clock has
gone off, repeat, the alarm clock has gone off. Please
make sure that all students report to their assigned
schools in time for the next semester. Confirm."

"Understood, Father," the voice replied. "All students
are to report to their schools immediately and deliver
their assignments."

"That is correct," Utkin replied. "I look forward to
seeing their grades."

"As do we," the voice on the other end said before
hanging up.

Utkin replaced the receiver, wiping it off with his
sleeve. Now that the operation had been set in motion,
he had a lot to do—starting with getting out of the city
within the next twelve hours.

2

Geneva, Switzerland
Two days later

Mustering every bit of her willpower, Kathri Brauer extricated herself from her lover's embrace and rolled out of bed. "What is the rush, my beauty? You still have plenty of time to make it to work." Alexei Panshin snaked a muscular, toned arm toward her leg. "Come back to bed for just a few minutes…"

Brauer looked down at him, nearly succumbing to her desire to just jump back into his arms. *God, I could just stare at him all day,* she thought, taking in his chiseled torso, strong legs and arms, and a face that could have graced the cover of a men's fashion magazine. Just the thought of how they'd been spending every night since they'd met five days ago almost made her knees buckle.

"That's tempting, but I won't be going anywhere if you keep that up."

Before her resolve could weaken any further, she hurried around the corner to the marble bathroom. Forgoing the whirlpool tub, she headed for the glassed-in waterfall shower and turned it on, luxuriating in the hot needle-like jets of water pouring over her. As she washed up, she thought of her new lover.

Alexei Panshin was a midlevel representative of a large import-export firm out of Saint Petersburg, looking to expand its reach around the world. He'd come to Geneva on a fact-finding mission to investigate various banking methods that might better serve his superiors back in Russia. Brauer had met him at a networking gala held in the Four Seasons Hotel des Bergues. As good as he looked naked, he almost looked even better in a tuxedo.

From the moment their gazes had met, it was as if fireworks had gone off. Brauer was more than experienced, having had a marriage, a divorce and several lovers under her belt, not to mention rising in the cutthroat world of international trade.

With her penetrating intelligence, five-eleven height, Nordic good looks and white-blond hair, Brauer knew she often came across as intimidating on a first meeting. But Alexei Panshin hadn't been intimidated in the least. When he first walked up to her bearing two glasses of champagne, the moment he opened his mouth, she was lost. The rest of the party fell away, and it was just the two of them, alone.

Several glasses of champagne later, they were making out in the back of the Mercedes-Benz S-Class sedan Panshin's company had provided to chauffeur him around the city. They'd ended up at his hotel, the luxurious Mandarin Oriental Geneva, and the rest of their time together had passed in a blur of incredible conversation, gourmet meals and mind-melting sex.

She got out of the shower and wrapped herself in a

huge, fluffy towel. Checking the time, she figured she would just make it if she didn't mind putting up with slightly damp hair on the way over.

Drying, dressing and applying her makeup in record time, she trotted out the door to find Panshin setting down his smartphone. He was sitting in front of two breakfasts on a tray—a full one for him, and a continental of croissants and fruit for her.

"That's so sweet of you." Even though it would put her behind, Brauer buttered a croissant. "Who called?"

"My company. They are impressed with what I have learned so far, and wish for me to stay in the city for a few more days—to better take advantage of the contacts I have made here." He rose and took her hands in his, kissing pastry crumbs off them. "But we can discuss that this evening. As much as it pains me to say it, you should probably get going, yes?"

Damn!

"Yes, I've got to run." She kissed him and turned to leave.

THE DRIVE TO the office seemed to take forever, and Brauer found it hard to concentrate on anything—paying attention to traffic, the emails she had her car's built-in system read to her on the way, the project she was supposed to be briefing her boss on this morning—all of it paled in comparison to her new, white-hot relationship.

Pulling into the underground garage, she got out of her car and trotted to the elevator. As she was getting in, her phone vibrated.

Conference moved up. Go directly to 15th floor conference room, the text read. Brauer knew she was supposed to stop on the main level and go through the security checkpoint, but she was already running close to her scheduled conference start time as it was, and stopping there would make her late. Besides, she had been working at the WTO building for the past four years—she certainly wouldn't risk destroying her career to smuggle in something. And no one else had gotten to her briefcase in all the time she'd had it, so when the elevator arrived, she got in and pushed the button for the fifteenth floor.

Grateful to find the elevator empty, Brauer took a few moments to run through the salient points of her presentation in her head, thanking her lucky stars she had been mostly done with it before she'd met Alexei.

The bell chimed, signaling she had reached her destination floor. Kathri stepped out and headed directly for the frosted glass conference room at the end of the corridor. She entered and blinked in surprise at seeing not only the CEO of the company, but also several board members.

"Ah, Ms. Brauer, so good to see you this morning," her boss, Loïc Gilliard, greeted her as he shook her hand. He quickly introduced her to the other board members. "We're looking forward to seeing what you have to show us today."

"And I think you'll be pleased with my recommendations, if you don't mind my saying so," she replied as she strode to the head of the table and set down her briefcase. "I'll just need a few moments to set up—"

As she reached for the locks, she noticed a new scratch marring the brass finish on the left one—the same one that had popped open back at the hotel room. I'll have to get that polished and fixed, she thought as she set the combination dials, undid the latches and opened the case. Or maybe just replace the whole damn thing—

The small bomb in her briefcase detonated with a

force powerful enough to blow her face off. She was blasted off her feet, hitting the wall hard enough to crack the wood before crashing to the floor. She had no idea that the explosion blew out all of the windows in the room and set the fire alarm blaring.

The bank's CEO, who had been walking over to stand next to Brauer, took the full force of the flying briefcase lid in the chest, pulverizing his ribs and stopping his heart. He was dead before he hit the floor.

With the blast directed more or less away from the board members, they escaped with their lives.

Amazingly, Brauer lived for one hundred twenty-two minutes after the blast. But as the paramedics were lifting her onto a gurney to take her to a medevac helicopter in a vain attempt to save her life, all she kept repeating was one word:

"Alexei..."

3

Stony Man Farm, Virginia
Twelve hours later

Head bobbing in time with the electronic dance music blasting through his earbuds, Akira Tokaido scanned the various monitors at his workstation. Although a genius computer hacker, the young man had quickly grown to love reviewing the endless data feeds. After all, what was data mining but searching for patterns in events and correlating the possible outcomes? In a way, he felt it was kind of like figuring out a program, but in real life.

However, real life was much more random and arbitrary. Just this morning, a bomb had gone off at the World Trade Organization headquarters in Geneva, Switzerland. Tokaido scanned the CIA summary document, learning that it seemed an employee had brought the explosives in with her, which explained how it had gotten by the main entry security. She had been killed in the blast, along with the current WTO chairman. Several board members had also been injured. No terrorist group had claimed responsibility yet, and police were pursuing all possible leads.

Tokaido flagged that as being of possible interest, then ran a search through domestic and international databases and law-enforcement files for acts classified as potential terrorism in the last thirty-six hours. More than eighty popped up, from a skirmish between the Sudanese People's Liberation Army and what looked like the last of the Anyayna II resistance in the Sudan to a disarmed bomb planted by a radical anarchist splinter group in Iceland to a raid on a known militia headquarters in Montana.

Next, he refined his search to the European continent and the United Kingdom, getting a dozen hits. These ranged from the small—a flaming garbage bin in Leicester, England—to the much more deadly: an assassination of a midlevel government official in Brussels, Belgium.

The Stony Man hacker skimmed through that one as well, and learned the victim, Jean-George Belloc, was the country's finance minister. He had been ambushed outside his home, shot in his car as he was heading to work. The suspect, driving a motorcycle, had worn a full-coverage helmet, and had made his escape before any eyewitnesses could get a good look at the assassin.

Pulling up recent quotes from the slain government official, Tokaido found he had been advocating taking a harder stance in trade negotiations with Russia, even suggesting the possibility of sanctions for its recent actions in the Ukraine, and its intervention in the Syrian civil war. Of course, that wasn't really anything new—most of the countries in the European Union weren't happy with Russia's recent saber-rattling, but they apparently also weren't going to speak too loudly about it, either, for fear of provoking the bear.

After all, look what happened to this guy, Tokaido mused.

On a hunch, he refined his search to potential terrorist acts with any links to Russia, adding his new target country to the list, in the event there had been any domestic incidents recently. His event list shrank to six: the Brussels event plus five others. Four of them he eliminated fairly quickly, although he did confirm that Polish authorities had finally captured a Lithuanian serial killer that had eluded them for the past decade. But the last one, occurring in Germany, made him frown as he studied it.

The percentage chance of this event being classified a terrorist act was small, but still viable. The body of a retired German army general had been found in his home the previous evening, apparently having died from a fall down his stairs. What made both him and the incident of interest was that he was a staunch opponent of friendly relations with Russia, and had written a book and several op-ed pieces critical of both his own government and Russia's. He had also received death threats from fringe groups seeking to normalize relations between the two countries.

So that's two with Russian connections…although the German one is thin at best, Tokaido thought. He returned to the first one, the Geneva bombing. More data had been aggregated on that case in just a past few minutes, including the last thing the woman said after the bomb had gone off. It was a man's name: Alexei.

The young hacker blinked. It was probably just coincidence, right? He hacked into the security cameras outside the WTO headquarters until he found her car entering the underground parking level. He then scanned all of the perimeter cameras in a five-minute window around her entrance to see if anything unusual came up. He watched intently, then expanded the time window to ten minutes, but nothing out of the ordinary appeared on the monitors.

Then Tokaido tried to see if her car had a GPS program he could use to backtrack the route she had used to drive to work. He managed to hack into the car, but the GPS wasn't activated. So he began backtracking her route by using the traffic cameras located on the main thoroughfares.

Even with the help of Stony Man's computers, it took him more than forty-five minutes to plot the route using the available cameras. But at last he had her route plotted from start to finish. And she had started from the Mandarin Oriental Geneva.

Tokaido whistled, then muttered, "I suppose a mid-level NGO functionary could splurge on a night at a fancy hotel, but I doubt that's what was happening."

The rest was all too easy. A check of the guest registry revealed that one—and only one—guest named Alexei, an Alexei Panshin, had been checked in for the past week. Video footage showed him moving about the hotel—including with the bomb victim. In fact, from what was revealed by the hallway cameras, they seemed to be having a very close relationship. And what was even more interesting, he had checked out of the hotel within twenty minutes of the WTO employee leaving. Unfortunately, video footage did not show his face.

There was, of course, one more thing to check. A quick search of public documents indicated a decisive cooling of the WTO toward doing business with Russia, with several interviews with the now-deceased CEO pointing toward a definite distancing of the organization from the country, citing its continuing record of corruption and human rights abuses. And countries around the world typically took the WTO's opinion on something—whether it was a trade agreement or an emerging country's potential market viability—pretty seriously.

But even so, did any of this actually mean anything? Alexei was a common enough name, particularly in Russia and Bulgaria. It was simply possible she was mouthing the name of her lover right before she died.

A quick cross-check on Alexei Panshin revealed that he was an employee of Artus International, an import-export firm based in Saint Petersburg, and that he had been on what looked like a business trip to Geneva. All fairly aboveboard, from what Tokaido could tell. Even so, the nagging suspicion about these seemingly unrelated events still wouldn't subside. It was possible that this man wasn't the real Alexei Panshin.

Though hacking was Tokaido's area of expertise, he had been encouraged to delve into data analysis. While training him in the cryptic art, his boss, Aaron "the Bear" Kurtzman, had stressed that it was as much art as science. "Connecting what seems like disparate events into a cohesive picture can often rely on your gut instinct as much as the hard data you acquire. The trick is knowing when to go with your feeling about a particular situation, and when to rely on the evidence as your primary lead."

With a sigh, Tokaido saved his data and rose from his chair to go find Kurtzman. Even if he was wrong about all of this, it would be a good theoretical exercise for them to discuss, and he could get some pointers to refine his analytical skills.

He was just heading for the main doors to the Computer Room when they slid open and Kurtzman wheeled himself into the room.

"Hey, Bear, I—" was all Tokaido said as he popped an earbud out to talk before he was forced to step out of the way of the other man as he zoomed his wheelchair over to his workstation.

"Akira, have you got anything unusual on the Russians this morning?" Kurtzman asked without even a perfunctory greeting as he began looking over his own monitors.

"I...well, I don't know if it's unusual, but I did notice what looked like some Federation-based activity over the past twenty-four hours. Why?"

"I want you to have whatever you've got ready to present in five minutes. A US senator was just shot and wounded in Paris an hour ago, and the assailant seemed to be of Russian origin. We want to know what's going on over there, and if it ties into anything larger, and if so, how."

"I'm on it." Tokaido ran back to his station and began typing with lightning speed.

"AND THOSE ARE the correlations between the various events, as I see them," Tokaido said, hoping he didn't sound too nervous.

Normally he served as support staff, assisting Mack Bolan or Able Team or Phoenix Force with their missions in the field. There, he was rock-solid, the calm voice in the team members' earpieces giving them up-to-the-minute security intel, or defeating a security system from the other side of the world.

He could count on one hand the number of times he'd actually been involved in presenting a briefing to the head of Stony Man Farm.

Currently, Hal Brognola was staring at him like a bulldog eyeing a particularly juicy steak. Tokaido didn't take it personally—he knew the big Fed regarded anyone who had what he wanted in exactly the same way. The Justice Department honcho was director of the clandestine Sensitive Operations Group, based at Stony Man Farm, and was Stony Man's conduit to the White House.

Tokaido shifted his gaze to Barbara Price, Stony Man's mission controller, the person who handled oversight of the Farm's missions. She nodded at him and smiled, indicating he'd done a good job on his summary presentation.

That was confirmed by Brognola. "Nice work, Akira. Good to see Bear's program is bearing some fruit.

"Okay, people, what does this seeming blitzkrieg of terror attacks mean? Are they really related, or are these just random acts that are occurring close enough together to draw our attention?"

"Given the increasing severity of the incidents, and the fact that Interpol, MI-5, and the Bundesamt für Verfassungsschutz have all gone to high alert internally, I don't see how we can't view this as anything but some kind of coordinated, if erratic, assault on the European Union as a whole," Kurtzman replied.

"And the US, don't forget." Brognola snatched the soggy cigar from his mouth and jabbed the unlit end at Kurtzman. "I never liked that pompous ass Richard DiStephano, but no one deserves to be shot."

"Says here that the assailant sped by on a motorcycle as DiStephano was heading to a meeting with his counterpart in the French government," Price said. "The attacker fired at least two dozen rounds from a small submachine gun as he sped by, hitting DiStephano and killing his aide."

"That's a damn shame," Kurtzman said. "What's DiStephano's prognosis?"

"Stable, although it was touch and go for a while," Price answered. "They say one of the gendarmes providing security wounded the shooter, making him crash his motorcycle, but he still got away."

Kurtzman grunted as he reviewed the data on the French attack. "DiStephano's one of those hawks beating the drum for military intervention in Sudan, isn't he?"

Brognola nodded sourly. "Yeah, mostly to counter what he feels is the increased Russian presence in the country. He's amassed a small group of right-wing chuckleheads—mostly first-termers—and they've been trying to fire up a larger coalition to put a bill forward to send troops over there. Of course, they're ignoring the very real threat of ISIS in the region, as well." He shook his head. "The damn fools spend as much time putting their collective feet in their mouths in the media as they do actual governance."

"Given the other attacks we've confirmed, this seems to link them all into a strong covert Russian operation," Kurtzman said.

"But to what end?" Price asked. "Several of these obvious links—that one or more of the supposed perpetrators behind these incidents may be of Russian origin—are still so weak that they might be a sophisticated ploy to fool us into thinking Moscow is behind all of this. What if we're looking at an elaborate false-flag operation meant to make us chase it back all the way to the Kremlin? With US-Russian relations so strained at the moment, we need to make absolutely sure that we're correct about our intelligence pointing to whoever's behind all of this."

"Barbara's absolutely right," the fifth member of the

conference said from the large monitor on the wall. "And the best way to do that is by putting some boots on the ground—mine."

Mack Bolan, aka the Executioner, was connected to the War Room via an encrypted satellite feed. He and Jack Grimaldi had been returning from a successful operation in northern Africa when this situation had arisen.

"Fortunately, we're not too far from Paris," Bolan said, "and I can begin my investigation there, since that has direct American involvement. Looks like we're about four hours away from Charles de Gaulle, so I'll have Jack drop me off, and I'll see if I can pick up the assassin's trail."

The Executioner picked up a tablet computer and flicked through the data he'd been sent. "DiStephano had been on his way to a meeting when he was assaulted. Are there any other events in the next twenty-four hours I need to be aware of, especially ones with high-value targets? Even wounded, this assassin may try to strike again if the payoff is of high enough value."

"Plus, given the timing of these incidents, we should assume we are dealing with at least three to five individuals," Price said. "It is possible that the wounded attacker won't even be there tonight but one or two of the others may be."

"How about a visit from the Austrian president?" Brognola asked. "He's in Paris, and what's more, he put out a statement saying he's not leaving until he's concluded his business with the French government—and guess what that is?"

"A conference to discuss a coordinated response to the recent aggressive actions of Russia?" Bolan replied.

"Jesus, what do you have over there, the meeting

itinerary?" Brognola asked. "That was almost word-for-word."

The black-haired man smiled. "What can I say, Hal. I've been listening to you gripe about the Foggy Bottom boys and their BS for too long."

"He just arrived this morning, and a welcoming dinner is planned at the Hôtel de Marigny, the traditional housing for visiting heads of state in France. It's right next to the Élysée Palace, so security will be heavy regardless. The event is scheduled to begin at 1900 local time this evening," Price told him.

"Well, considering we still don't have a solid lead on any of these operatives, even with their previous assault, right now they still possess the element of surprise," Bolan said. "And if they're still in the area, the chance to take down a sitting president is something they probably won't pass up."

"We'll make sure you're added to the guest list and we'll alert both Interpol and French intelligence, who will be overjoyed to see you, I'm sure," Price said.

"As long as we can take down these bastards, I don't care who I have to work with to get the job done."

4

Avenue des Champs-Élysées
Paris, France

Alexei Panshin drove the Renault sedan through the narrow streets with ease, staying within a few miles of the posted speed limit, following every traffic law, alert to the occasional uniformed police officer directing traffic through a particularly busy intersection. If he and his companions had been stopped, the officer doing so would have had a career-making arrest, given the various weapons and other illegal equipment inside.

Assuming he survived the encounter, of course.

As he drove, eyes flicking from one side of the street to the other, Panshin said, "You both have the plan and timetable down?"

"Yes, Alexei, we will be there with plenty of time to set up what we need," the slender woman in the passenger seat replied. Of a similar build and general appearance to the man beside her, the woman, Amani Nejem, also swept her gaze across their surroundings, missing nothing.

Panshin looked into the small rearview mirror, and met the gaze of Nejem's backup, Kisu Darsi, staring back at him. "Don't worry about me, Alexei. I'm not even feeling any pain."

The team leader's eyes flashed. "You're just fortunate we were able to get the bullet out. You are certain you can complete this operation?"

Still holding his gaze, Darsi raised his left arm until it was outstretched and level with his shoulder—something he shouldn't have been able to do, given that three hours earlier there had been two bullets in his upper chest. But he evinced no sign of discomfort as he did so.

"All right, then. You both know where you are supposed to be," he said as he pulled the car over in a neighborhood of converted apartment buildings. "I will see you both there."

Panshin got out, and moments later Nejem was behind the wheel and the sedan was pulling away, heading toward the hotel that would host the state dinner. Casually looking around as he headed to a structure at the end of the block, Panshin made sure no one was taking any interest in him as he walked up the steps to a four-story apartment building and tried the electronically locked door. It didn't budge.

Panshin thought about trying to contact his target through the intercom, but decided against it, as he didn't want to risk spooking him. Instead, he pulled a trick he had been assured would work in neighborhoods like these, filled with students and young, working-class professionals. He simply ran his hand down the entire line of intercom buttons.

Within seconds, one of them buzzed the door, and he

opened it and slipped inside. His target's apartment was on the top floor, and Panshin took the stairs, not wanting to be seen by others in the building. He reached the floor quickly and started down the hallway until he found the door he was looking for. After glancing to the right and left to make sure no one was around, he knocked softly.

The muffled sounds of movement came from inside. "Who is it?" an annoyed voice asked in French.

"It's Reynard," Panshin answered, giving the name of one of the apartment dweller's coworkers.

"Reynard?" A chain rattled on the other side, and the door cracked open. A young man peered at him. "What do you— Wait, who are you?"

By then it was too late. As the young man struggled to make sense of the man who was nearly a mirror image of himself, Panshin grabbed the edge of the door and pushed hard.

It wasn't a big movement, but it was enough to tear the chain from the wall and shove the boxers-clad man back from the door, sending him stumbling into the high-ceilinged one-bedroom apartment. His butt hit the stained Formica counter that framed part of the kitchen, and he winced even as he threw up an arm to try to fend off this unknown assailant.

"Hey—" was all he got out before Panshin had closed the door and was on him, moving so fast his quarry appeared to be crying out in slow motion. One lightning-fast hand batted aside his upraised arm, and Panshin's other hand, fingers curled into a tight ram's head position, shot forward into the man's throat, crushing his larynx.

The effect was immediate. Gasping, the young man grabbed his injured neck as his windpipe swelled and closed, cutting off the flow of air to his lungs. Mouth opening and closing helplessly, he sank to his knees, face reddening as his brain became starved for oxygen. He grabbed at Panshin, who sidestepped him and let the dying man fall to the floor, where he thrashed helplessly and clutched at his throat before falling unconscious.

A startled yelp alerted him to the presence of someone else in the apartment. Panshin looked up to see a young woman in a spaghetti-strap tank top and panties staring back at him, a look of openmouthed horror on her face. He cursed inwardly. All of their surveillance data indicated the target should have been alone today.

As he started for her, the woman whirled and darted back into the bedroom, slamming the heavy door in Panshin's face. He hit it with his shoulder just as she turned the lock. Stepping back, he raised a leg and pistoned it into the doorknob, smashing it apart, but the door still held. Cursing, he hit the same spot again, this time shoving the door open hard enough for it to fly into the bedroom wall and smash a hole in the plaster.

Panshin shot inside and saw the open window in the larger dormer. Running to it, he saw the woman, now dressed in a leather jacket and combat boots, carefully moving across the roof toward the next building. A feral grin creasing his face, he stepped out and gave chase, cursing her for putting him behind schedule, knowing every second counted now.

She had a decent lead, but for him, walking the three-inch pathway around the sloped roof was as easy as walking across a street, and he soon closed the gap. She glanced over her shoulder to see him gaining fast, and that knowledge spurred her to greater speed—straight toward the narrow alley between that building and the next. Fortunately, she was running too hard to draw enough breath to scream for help.

Panshin ran faster as well, wanting to cut her off before she leaped, but he just missed her, his fingers brushing her jacket as she desperately soared through the air. She landed hard and rolled, losing one boot, but was up and running again within moments.

He backed up a few steps, then accelerated to his top speed, easily leaping the three-yard gap with a few feet to spare. Unlike his quarry, he landed on his feet and kept running, easily catching up to her.

When his right hand grabbed her neck, the woman opened her mouth to scream, but he quickly cut her off by the simple expedient of clapping his left hand over her mouth and nose. Already panting from fear and the chase, with her air cut off, she panicked completely, tearing and beating at his iron-like hands as he dragged her out of sight behind a large air-conditioning unit.

Already her struggles were weakening, but Panshin didn't let his guard down, and made sure she didn't reach his face with her nails by using the hand that had been holding her neck to pin her arms—anything out of the ordinary now could interfere with the mission. He maintained his hold until she passed out, then carried her to the back side of the building and peeked over the side.

As he'd hoped, it was a narrow backstreet filled with trash receptacles and piled bags of refuse. With a quick look around to ensure that no one was watching, he grabbed her by the legs and held her upside down over a section of alley that was clear of garbage, then let her go, not even waiting for the impact of her head on the pavement to reach him. Her death was a foregone conclusion.

At the edge of the building, he made sure to find the loose boot and toss it toward where he'd dropped the woman. At this point, it didn't matter if it also fell off the roof or stayed where he'd tossed it. Now it was just a clue pointing toward a young woman committing suicide.

He jumped back to the other building, reentered the apartment, closing and locking the window behind him, and walked to the closet. Hanging in a black garment bag was his disguise for the evening. Quick searches of the nightstand and the body produced the final pieces—Yves Montauk's smartphone, his billfold with his driver's license, and a government identification badge that would allow Panshin access to the Élysée Palace and the Hôtel de Marigny.

5

General Directorate for
Internal Security Headquarters
Levallois-Perret, France

"Look, we can sit around here for the next ninety minutes or so and argue jurisdictions and whatnot, but the evidence we've obtained—and already made available to your department—indicates that the Austrian president is at risk of an assassination attempt tonight, and I plan to be there, with or without your government's approval."

"Be that as it may, Agent Cooper, our security has already been doubled for the function," Captain Bellamy Lambert, of the Terrorism Department of the Direction générale de la sécurité intérieure—DGSI—replied. "Our people are among the best in the world at what they do, and I have no doubt that the president and the rest of the guests will be safe under their watch."

The brown-haired man cleared his throat. "And while we appreciate your government's sharing of the data you have uncovered, as far as I know, you are here to investigate the attack on Richard DiStephano earlier today. So then, by all means, please do so, and let us handle tonight's event. Your presence there would be unnecessary, and even detrimental to our own established security protocols. It would be as if we had showed up to your White House and demanded to oversee the security details for your own President—hardly acceptable, *n'est pas*?"

He leaned forward on the desk and speared Mack Bolan with his dark blue eyes. "If you do show up there tonight, you will be escorted off the premises. If you attempt to detain or arrest anyone on the premises, you will be arrested instead."

Bolan blew out an exasperated breath. Bureaucratic red tape was to be expected, but at this level, it was hard to stomach. The fight against terrorism was a global one, and for the most part, cooperation between countries was usually a given. However, in every counterterrorist organization, there were always those people either more interested in following the letter of the law, unwilling to accept that their own country's resources weren't up to handling a possible threat, or trying to protect whatever little fiefdom they'd carved out within the organization. Bolan was pretty sure Captain Lambert was a combination of the first two.

"Captain, I've been trying to tell you for the past ten minutes that every indicator we've found shows that that the two events are related. The same assassins who tried to kill Richard DiStephano will attempt to assassinate the Austrian president tonight. Let me help you catch them."

"And if they do try anything, which sounds most incredible, given the failed attack on your own senator, we will apprehend them. Please, Agent Cooper, there is no need for your assistance this evening—" The DGSI officer was interrupted by his desk phone ringing. *"Excusez-moi."*

Bolan leaned back in his chair and regarded the other man steadily while he picked up the phone. He had an idea as to the nature of the call, and while he'd hoped he wouldn't have to use the option, preferring to operate in cooperation with local law enforcement whenever possible, Lambert had left him no choice.

"Oui…oui…" The captain's eyes widened as they flicked to Bolan, then he scowled. *"Oui…oui, Minister, je comprend."* He jerked the phone away from his ear, looked at it for a moment, then set it back in its cradle. When he looked back up at Bolan, his gaze was, if anything, even steelier.

"Exactly what department of American law enforcement are you with again, Agent Cooper?"

"The Justice Department."

"Hmm… I would have thought this would be a State Department matter, the FBI, or perhaps even CIA…" Lambert cleared his throat again, but Bolan didn't even twitch at the so-called bait dangling out there.

"Regardless, the minister of my department has just informed me that I am to extend any and all assistance to you in your investigation, including a suitable escort to guide you around the city. I have selected just the officer to help you in this matter." He picked up his phone again, punched in a number and spoke a few rapid-fire sentences to the person on the other end of the line. He hung up and addressed Bolan.

"Sergeant Palomer will be awaiting you in the foyer. If there is anything else my department can assist you with, she will also be your liaison. Good luck, Agent Cooper."

"Thank you." With a nod, Bolan stood and let himself out into the hallway, retracing his steps back to the main entry of the DGSI headquarters.

"Agent Matthew Cooper?"

Bolan glanced to his left, where the query had come from, and saw a petite woman with dark brown hair pulled back in a ponytail. She acknowledged him with a curt nod. "I am Sergeant Marie Palomer, assigned to assist you in this case. Where would you like to begin?"

"How familiar are you with the situation?" Bolan asked as he began walking toward the front door again.

She fell in beside him. "I have been briefed on the attack on your Senator DiStephano. That is the incident we are investigating, correct?"

"Not tonight," Bolan replied as they walked outside and toward a black Range Rover on loan from the US Embassy. "Do you have formal wear?"

"I can pull something together," she said with only a slight pause. "May I ask why?"

"Because tonight we're attending the state dinner welcoming the Austrian president to your country," Bolan said as he opened the passenger door for her. "With any luck, we'll be there to prevent his assassination.

"But first, we have to stop and pick up my tuxedo."

"Yves Montauk," now impeccably dressed in his serving tuxedo, got off the bus on the Champs-Élysées and slowly walked the last half mile to his destination, smoking a cigarette along the way, enjoying the smooth blend of tobacco, so much better than what he could get back home in Russia.

He took the opportunity to sight out the primary and secondary escape routes they would use to get clear of the building once the assassination had occurred. Due to the more public nature of this event, they were planning a more subtle attack by using poison this time. By the time the Austrian president began to feel the effects, ideally Panshin's team would be long gone, heading on to the next target.

Flicking away the butt of his cigarette, Panshin walked down the Avenue de Marigny and around to the side, where the staff entrance was located. He submitted to the identification check and the metal detector scan before his ID was returned to him and he was allowed to head down to the basement, where the kitchen, food prep and laundry were located.

As he ambled toward the staff elevator, Panshin took a few moments to get the lay of the land, ensuring that the plans he'd memorized matched what he was seeing on the inside. So far, everything looked exactly as it should.

"What the hell are you doing here, Yves?" a jocular voice said loudly from behind him, making him freeze for the barest moment before turning to the speaker with a wide smile.

"What are you talking about? I am here to work, of course." Panshin was careful to add the northern Bretagne accent to his French, speaking just like Yves would have.

The other man, a headwaiter Panshin's files identified as Henri Latrec, chuckled. "I know, but you are early. The Yves I know always arrives a minute before the serving is to begin, if I am lucky. Could it be that you are finally turning over a new leaf?"

Panshin kept his smile in place, although inwardly

he was cursing the other man's chronic near-lateness—again, anything out of the ordinary might be seen as a red flag by an alert guard or staff person. Having trained since birth to flawlessly insinuate himself into any scenario, the slightest slipup could result in blowing the entire mission.

But even as Panshin considered whether he would have to kill the man, his smile didn't slip a bit as he nodded. "Perhaps I am, Henri, perhaps I am."

"Good Lord! I think the world may be ending!" Throwing a meaty arm around Panshin's shoulders, the headwaiter steered him toward the elevator. "Despite your constant appearing here in the nick of time, you are still one of my best servers, which is good, because I would hate to have to let you go!" He clapped him on the shoulder as the elevator dinged. "Go wash up. We are about to begin the reception, and canapés will be served in ten minutes. I will see you in the reception room."

"Thank you, Henri," Panshin replied as he stepped into the small box. "I'll be there immediately."

Once alone, he did not betray a bit of elation at pulling off the impersonation with someone who obviously knew his dead counterpart very well. They already looked fairly similar, and judicious disguise work and makeup had turned him into an almost exact duplicate of the other man. Perhaps this would be easier than he thought.

He stepped into the washroom, removed his jacket and rolled up his sleeves to scrub his hands and forearms. When done, he redressed, checking the bottom seam of the tuxedo jacket to ensure that the poison he intended to use on the Austrian president was still secure, yet easily reachable.

Taking a last look at himself in the mirror, Panshin

smoothed back his black hair, straightened his bow tie, shot his cuffs and walked out to join the rest of the black-suited throng assembling to serve the various heads of the French government and their guests.

Before this night is over, he thought as he insinuated himself among them, we will have struck another blow for the motherland, and these soft, babbling fools will have learned another lesson in respect.

6

"If you keep pulling at that collar, you're going to dislodge the tie, which won't look very good at all."

Bolan dropped his finger from the constricting clothing and glanced ruefully at Palomer, who was sitting comfortably in the driver's seat. "Is it that obvious?"

"That you do not enjoy formal evening wear? Quite." She glanced at him with a smile. "If you don't mind my saying so, however, you look remarkable."

"Thank you." Bolan had been able to visit a tailor who was an American asset. He had obtained a tuxedo that was well fitted, yet cut loose enough to conceal his pistol in a pancake holster that rode at the small of his back.

"Well, it's supposed to make me blend in with the crowd, so hopefully it will do the job. But you're right. I'm more a sport coat and slacks kind of guy." Bolan eyed her again. "If you don't mind my saying so, that is quite the evening wear on a sergeant's salary."

After he had gotten dressed, they'd swung by her apartment, where the sergeant had run inside and come back out in ten minutes dressed in an emerald green, floor-length, elegantly shimmering gown. With time running out, she had offered to drive, and he'd taken her up on it, figuring she'd be better able to smooth over any traffic issues if they were stopped along the way.

"Glad you like it." She smiled. "I made it myself."

He raised an eyebrow. "A woman of many talents. How long have you been with the DGSI?"

"Four years, but I just made sergeant last year, so I've been in this position for almost eleven months."

Bolan had no idea what the qualifications were for sergeants in the DGSI. Palomer looked and sounded competent, but appearance was one thing, performance in the field was quite another. "What do you think of your current assignment?"

She stared straight ahead at the traffic. "As per my superior's orders, I am to give any and all assistance to you—as long as you are not about to break any of our laws, of course."

"Of course. Is Lambert your supervisor?"

She nodded. "I report directly to him."

Bolan nodded. "He struck me as fairly bureaucratic."

He was gratified to see a faint smile curve her lips up, accompanied by a classic Gallic shrug. "He is a good administrator. That is where he excels. But changes in his routine—especially unexpected ones, like you—those he doesn't handle as well."

"So, what is your opinion of this assignment?"

She glanced sidelong at him. "I believe that you already asked that."

"Not exactly. Before, I asked what you thought of this assignment. Now I'm asking your opinion of it."

"My opinion, Agent Cooper, is that I have been assigned to watch you to insure that you do not interfere with tonight's event. Technically, one could call this busywork, as the people overseeing security at the Hôtel de Marigny are among the very best in the world, and I have every confidence that if there is to be an assassin there, the person will be caught before he or she can do anything. However, I have my orders, and I will follow them to the best of my ability."

Bolan nodded again. "Excellent. That's all I could have asked of anyone assigned to me. It's my sincerest hope that the event goes off without a hitch, and you and I just get to stand around all night watching diplomats and other important people exchange small talk and drink expensive wine."

Making a final turn, Palomer nodded at the imposing stone edifice on their right, its stone driveway buried under limousines. "We're here."

They drove past the large main building with a two-story wing at a right angle to the rest of the structure. A steady stream of well-dressed men and women were entering the main lobby. Bolan glimpsed several people who looked like law enforcement handling crowd control.

"Which reception area is the event being held in?" Bolan asked, although he already knew.

"Salon A, the smaller of the two, below the raised ground floor," Palomer replied as she turned into a side parking lot that held several black Range Rovers and Mercedes-Benz SUVs. "Attendance should be about seventy-five to ninety people total, with an equal number of waitstaff."

"All of whom have been thoroughly vetted before tonight's event?"

She nodded. "As both Captain Lambert and I have already said, security has been heightened since the assault on Senator DiStephano. I have no doubt they've missed nothing."

"I certainly hope so," Bolan said.

Palomer parked their charcoal-gray Range Rover, and they both got out and walked around the corner to the rear of the structure, where an imposing steel door blocked their way. The sergeant knocked on it, and a few moments later it opened, and a bleary-looking man with a scattering of salt-and-pepper stubble on his cheeks peered at them. Despite his haggard facial appearance, his white dress shirt looked freshly pressed, and his tailored suit jacket was unwrinkled. *"Oui?"*

She showed her badge and introduced herself and Bolan, who had gotten out his Department of Justice identification and held it up for the man to see. He stared at it with a puzzled frown.

"What is the American DOJ doing here?" he asked in accented English.

"Investigation of an assault on a United States senator," Bolan said. "We have reason to believe that the perpetrators will strike here as well."

"Of course. I was sorry to hear of Senator DiStephano's injury, and hope he enjoys a speedy recovery."

"If you check your guest list, you'll see that Agent Matthew Cooper is on it, cleared by the minister himself," Palomer said. "We are to extend every courtesy."

"I'm primarily here in an observational capacity," Bolan added. He left out that the switch from observation to action could come at a moment's notice.

The man had already pulled out a smartphone and speed-dialed a number. Rapid French followed, with the man nodding as he spoke.

The man put his phone away and stuck out his hand. "I'm Alain Deschaines, head of security at the hotel.

Come on in. It never hurts to have two more sets of eyes on the premises."

He waved them inside and closed the heavy steel door behind them, making sure the electronic lock had engaged. "The reception is just starting, and a half dozen of my men and woman are mingling with the arriving guests right now. Do you suspect something will be attempted during that portion of the evening, or later?"

"It's hard to say," Bolan answered. "Political assassins typically want to draw as much attention to the kill as possible, so striking during the reception isn't likely, as the incident could be minimized and concealed without too much difficulty. I expect they'll try something during dinner, or perhaps during remarks afterward. In any event, I'd like to get a quick tour and take a look at your security facilities, and then I think the best place to be for the rest of the evening would be on the floor itself—with your permission."

Deschaines nodded as Bolan spoke. "While I do not have any general issue with that plan, my only concern would be if you inadvertently get in the way of one of my own people—no offense intended."

"No, I understand completely, and plan to be on-scene in an eyes-only capacity," Bolan replied. "Since time is of the essence, why don't we continue our conversation on the way to your security room?"

"Of course, right this way. Let me take you through the kitchen, in case there is anything you wish to see there."

Bolan and Palomer followed Deschaines down a plain gray stairwell and into a narrow corridor filled with wheeled serving racks and other kitchen appliances. It was hotter and more humid down there, and as they walked down the short passageway, they could hear the conversations and shouts of men and women working among the clatter and roar and chop of metal and wood and fire. A delicious mélange of smells, from roasting meat to a creamy sauce to some short of sharp yet fragrant spice, all combined to somehow create a delicious harmony for the nose.

"Our kitchen houses forty people, from line chefs to pastry chefs and everything in between," the head of security said as they entered the huge room filled with stainless-steel ovens, large gas-burning stoves and long steel countertops where a veritable white-clad army was busy preparing the evening's repast.

Deschaines pointed to the figure of a man wreathed in steam and smoke doing at least three things at once while instructing two other people. "I'd introduce you to the head chef, but he'd likely bite my head off at the moment. Regardless, everyone here has been working for the hotel for at least five years, and their credentials are impeccable."

His attention was drawn to one of the servers, a tall, black-haired man walking by pushing one of the loaded serving racks. "Yves, a moment?"

The man stopped and eyed the three people curiously. "Yes, sir?"

Deschaines patted his pocket. "I heard a beeping on you somewhere." He pulled out a smartphone. "You know the rules. All phones are to be off during serving hours."

The man ducked his head in an abashed nod. "Yes, sir, sorry." He touched a switch on the side of the device. "It won't happen again, sir."

"See that it does not. Carry on." Dismissing the server with a wave, Deschaines gestured for Bolan and Palomer to follow him.

"Anything out of the ordinary tonight in the run-up to the event?" Bolan asked as they stopped for and dodged sweating, harried cooks and waitstaff while negotiating their way across the bustling room. Along the way, he kept a sharp eye out for anyone that looked out of the ordinary—someone watching their surroundings more than what they were supposed to be doing, or someone who didn't seem to know what they were doing in the first place. But it looked like everyone was where they were supposed to be, doing what they were supposed to be doing, so no luck spotting the assassin—or assassins, he reminded himself—here.

"Nothing more than usual," Deschaines replied. "Two of our people called in sick, so we activated a couple of reserve personnel, both of whom have many years of experience. With a staff this large, it's quite rare that the lineup stays the same each night, but no, nothing out of the ordinary."

The man's answer didn't reassure Bolan—it made him more alert. Any skilled assassin would be a master at blending into his or her environment, remaining unobtrusive until it was time to make a move. And with more than two hundred people to try to keep an eye on, the chance was very minuscule that they would be able to stop the assassin before he or she struck. At best, it would have to be an intercept of the attempt—to the point of taking a bullet for the Austrian president if necessary.

"Here we are." Deschaines ran a card through a reader, pressed his thumb on a scanning pad and punched in a series of numbers to the steel-framed security entrance. The door was bank-vault thick as well, and slid into the wall to allow entry. Inside, three men and a woman sat before a bank of monitors, taking check-in calls while observing the ground floor, kitchen, and the ongoing event through three dozen monitors.

"Each individual member has his or her own code to access portions of the building as needed, and you saw the three steps I had to take to access the main room, so it would be very difficult for someone to pose as one of my personnel and gain access. Our protocols are reviewed and updated as needed every six months," Deschaines said while glancing over the monitors covering the reception for the president. Both he and the French president were in a receiving line, shaking hands with diplomats—including the current one from Russia to France, Bolan noted—ministers of the president's council, as well as underlings of theirs, influential businessmen, and others who ranked highly enough to receive a coveted invitation. Everyone was dressed to the nines, in formal wear and evening gowns, while black-jacketed men and women walked among them, offering trays of hors d'oeuvres and flutes of champagne.

"So many people," Palomer said as she took in the large scene of talking, laughing, drinking, eating attendees. "Where are we going to begin?"

"As close to ground zero as possible," Bolan replied before raising his voice slightly. "Alain, your people have this well in hand. Let's head down to the floor and get a closer look at what's going on there."

As Deschaines led them to the elevator, Bolan made sure his jacket was loose enough to allow easy access to his pistol, while hoping he wouldn't have to use it.

7

Charles de Gaulle Airport
Outside Paris, France

Mikhail Sevaron stepped off the Aeroflot jet into the airport with his small carry-on slung over his shoulder.

In his button-down white shirt and slacks, he might have been just another European business traveler. But his eyes—flat, cold, slate gray and missing nothing—told a different story to anyone who might care to give him a more than casual glance. They were the eyes of a killer.

In the terminal, he met with the three other members of his team, who had all arrived on different flights that day, and they exited the airport, heading to a sleek Mercedes-Benz limousine.

A balding, portly man in a rumpled suit, his forehead sweating slightly, sat inside, nodding to them as they entered and sat. Once the three men and one woman were all inside, the suited man waved the driver to go as soon as the door closed.

"The equipment you requested." He nodded at the four bulky diplomatic pouches on the seats.

Sevaron opened his pouch to find a .40-caliber HK P30 pistol, three magazines, a sound suppressor, a holster, a new passport, a driver's license, credit cards and money. He placed his own identification in the pouch, resealed it and handed it over to the portly man, as did his three companions. Barely glancing at the documentation, he worked the pistol's action, checking the barrel and muzzle, then tested its weight in his hand. With a shrug, he set the weapon in his lap and raised his gaze to the suited man across from him.

"What is our status?"

The man mopped his forehead with a linen handkerchief, even though the air-conditioning was on. "There have been no new incidents since the one with the US senator yesterday. Our people have been watching the airport, and train and bus stations since we received word of the assassination in Brussels. There has been no sighting of any of them."

Sevaron nodded. "Unsurprising. Utkin trained them to be the very best, after all. There's been no word on his whereabouts either, I take it?"

The other man shook his head. "He was last sighted boarding the Siberian Express, but agents on the train lost him during the Moscow-Yaroslavl leg, even though there were no stops. They say he escaped their surveillance just long enough to jump off the train on one of the sharper curves. Military units have already converged on the route and are searching for him as we speak, but if there was a vehicle waiting for him, he's probably long gone by now."

Sevaron cocked his head. The old scientist was bolder than expected. Well, maybe not, he thought. After all, he's the one who'd unleashed this killing spree all over Europe.

"Our report stated that one of the operatives sighted here was wounded in the attempt on the American. No hospital reports of gunshot injuries received?"

"Not even the slightest indication of one," the sweating man replied. "Remember, they have all been trained to be as self-reliant as possible. And given their…modifications, any injury sustained would have to be severe for them to even risk going to a hospital and being found out for what they truly are."

"An excellent point." Sevaron glanced out the window at the Paris scenery blurring by. "So, you still believe they are in the city?"

"At least one remains. Perhaps the others have moved on, I don't know." The other man leaned forward. "With their skills and abilities, they are like damnable ghosts, able to come and go as they please, with us grasping fruitlessly at the mere traces of their passing."

"Yet…" Sevaron trailed off.

"Yet I think they are still here. Not for long—another eight, ten hours at the most. You may even call me crazy, but I actually think they are planning another strike." He handed the man a piece of paper with the title *Reception and Dinner—Austrian President—Hôtel de Marigny* at the top, then leaned back in his seat.

Sevaron scanned the contents of the page, then handed it to his female team member, who glanced at it once, then handed it back.

"This event has already begun," he said. "Once we have our own transportation, we will go there. We will observe the building. If something happens, we will be on hand to apprehend the targets. Who knows? Maybe they will eliminate our Austrian problem before we can stop them."

The sweating man held up a finger. "We *cannot* have that happen! Utkin's people are at risk of upsetting plans that have been years in the making. To draw attention to ourselves now from other governments or international organizations would be the worst possible outcome."

"Understood. And what about local law enforcement?" Sevaron asked. "Most likely they are on a higher alert now, particularly given the incident with the American. How would you prefer that we deal with them if they get in our way?"

"*We* would prefer that you minimize your interactions with them as much as possible. However, the primary mission parameters take precedence over all other considerations."

The sweating man leaned forward again, making sure to hold Sevaron's full attention. "Find them and kill them *before* they assassinate the Austrian president. That is your *only* concern."

BY THE TIME Panshin made his third trip from the kitchen up to the reception floor, guests were already heading into an adjoining room to be seated for dinner. He walked around, offering guests a tray of salmon canapés.

But all the while he was serving, his mind was racing. It wasn't that he had nearly been busted for the turned-on smartphone, although that had been a very worrisome minute or two. It was seeing the two other people who had been with the head of security, as both of them screamed *outside police officer*.

Well, that wasn't quite true. The woman had screamed police officer, right down to her out-of-place posture, as if subconsciously she knew she didn't belong among the others she was guarding, no matter how well she tried to blend in. A passing glance wouldn't have caught it, but Panshin's training had included years of observation of body language and subconscious cues, to the point where it was second nature.

All of which made the black-haired man even more unusual. He was dressed perfectly, wearing the tuxedo with authority. He didn't fit in here, either. However, Panshin knew the type. The man had come to the hotel for a purpose, and he wasn't going to stop until he had achieved his goal, whatever it was.

And Panshin knew instinctively that he was there to stop them.

The man's ice-blue eyes had seemed to take in everything at once, and when their gazes locked for a moment, Panshin was almost certain the man could see right inside him, and knew he was an impostor. But his supreme control and training had won out, and the other man hadn't raised the alarm. However, he was still around somewhere, prowling the area. He would bear watching.

Panshin looked around for his backup team, wanting to let them know about the possible complication. While he could have ducked away and texted both of them, they had all been concerned about the security eavesdropping on cell phone transmissions, and didn't want to take the chance. Unfortunately, he didn't spot them right away, and his tray was rapidly becoming depleted. If he was caught on the floor with an empty tray for more than a few seconds, that would not go well.

He was heading back to the exit when a hand reaching for his tray caught his eye, and he stopped to let the guests help themselves. "These little salmon things are delicious, aren't they?" a familiar voice asked. "Do tell me what's in them, please?"

Panshin looked up to see Amani Nejem's smiling eyes looking back at him as she nibbled on the hors d'oeuvre. Kisu Darsi flanked her, their Al-Jazeera press badges prominently displayed.

He nodded at them. "Of course, *mademoiselle*. They are a specialty of our chef." He stepped closer, appearing to share the appetizer's ingredients. "I've seen a man who bears watching here. He is with a woman—" Panshin gave a quick description of her "—but she is not the main threat. He has black hair, blue eyes, about six feet two inches tall, maybe 220 pounds, midnight blue tuxedo, definitely armed. You will know him when you see him. He moves like one of us."

Nejem betrayed no hint of surprise, just nodded. "Outsider? From where?" she asked.

"I do not know. Possibly an American, arriving here after the earlier attack."

"Do we continue?"

Panshin nodded. "We will never get a better chance. I must go now. Be ready, and watch out for him. He must not interfere."

"Of course he won't," Darsi said as he snatched the last salmon snack from the tray. "Now go and fetch some more of these."

Although tempted to sneer at the other man, Panshin simply nodded and headed back to the kitchen for another tray, ready to begin the next stage of their mission.

WHEN BOLAN AND PALOMER reached the marble floor of the reception room, it was mostly empty, except for a few stragglers and members of the press who had somehow wrangled invitations.

"How do you want to play this?" he asked his companion.

She looked at Bolan, obviously surprised that he was asking her opinion. "Well, we should probably sweep the dining room for anything out of the ordinary. How about we split up and each take half of the room? With most of the people already seated, it shouldn't be a problem seeing the whole place."

"Sounds good to me. Why don't you go left, and I'll go right," Bolan said. "Casually sweep the entire perimeter and meet back at the entrance, so we can double-check each other's space, just in case."

"All right, meet you back here in a few minutes."

Bolan glanced at the entrance to see the last people heading inside. "Go in first. I don't want to draw attention to us by coming in together. I'll be a few seconds behind you."

She nodded and walked inside, following the reporters. Bolan hung back to make sure he was alone, then casually spoke to the empty air.

"Striker to Stony Base, Striker to Stony Base."

"Striker, this is Stony Base, read you loud and clear," Akira Tokaido's voice said through the miniature earpiece in his ear. Sophisticated, state-of-the-art, ultra-encrypted wireless technology allowed Bolan to be in contact with the Farm on the other side of the Atlantic without having to show a wire or any other piece of instantly identifiable equipment. "You're certainly putting on the Ritz tonight."

"Caviar and stuffed suits, more like it," Bolan replied. "Have you gotten anything off the footage yet?"

Along with his transceiver, the second button of his shirt contained a tiny camera. Bolan had been panning-and-scanning from the moment he'd entered the building, with the footage automatically transmitted through his smartphone via satellite back to Tokaido, who was trying to identify the faces through a computer search.

"That's a negative for the moment. Just a whole lot of people whose net worth exceeds mine by a few hundred million dollars or euros, or whatever they use for money over there—probably their firstborn children."

Bolan smiled as he strolled toward the dining hall. "And yet I'd rather have you at my back any day. I'm entering the main hall now, so prepare to get a lot more faces to process. If you find anything unusual, let me know, okay?"

"You got it, Striker. Stony Base out."

Bolan walked into the dining hall, which was a study in understated opulence. Glittering chandeliers cast a subdued, golden light over the entire room. The tables and chairs weren't the standard conference room plastic and vinyl. They were hardwood and plush, and looked very comfortable.

The tables had been arranged in a large U-shape, with the open end facing a small dais with a lectern and more tables on either side. Guests were seated both on the outside and inside, and lively conversation filled the hall. The servers continued shuttling back and forth, already setting out still-warm bread, crackers and caviar to start the evening. A half dozen serious-faced, alert men and women in somber business suits and obvious earpieces were spaced evenly around the room, two to a wall. Alain Deschaines had notified his people about Bolan and Palomer's arrival, so they did nothing to acknowledge him as he passed.

A balding man in a three-piece suit rose and walked to the lectern to say a few words to the assembled guests. Though he had a decent understanding of French, Bolan didn't pay a lot of attention to the opening remarks, as his gaze was on the guests, the waitstaff, even the security, looking for that one clue that would give him the identity of the assassin. If he could pick out the person, he'd be halfway to stopping the plan, rather than having to wait to react to whatever went down.

But as he walked and looked around, Bolan didn't see anyone acting the slightest bit out of the ordinary. He continued on his sweep, hoping to get an update from Tokaido that would enable him to spring into action, or maybe Palomer had spotted something during her sweep.

As he approached the halfway point of the perimeter, he saw the sergeant walking toward him. She shook her head minutely. Nothing spotted on her end.

Where the hell was he? Bolan thought. And how would he make his move?

8

Panshin was becoming concerned. There didn't seem to be any way he could get at the president's courses.

The problem was Marcel. He was the top server at the hotel, and Henri had tasked him with serving the president's table. They were about to serve the first course, the soup, which would work the best with his poison, as the cream base would cover any possible unusual odor or taste. The problem was that Marcel was either always at his station, or one of the cooks was there, putting final garnishes on the bowls, arranging things, and basically being in the way. Panshin couldn't get close enough without being spotted.

Then he saw his chance, although he'd have to time it just right. Taking his own tray of soup bowls, he started toward the exit as Marcel was coming in. Then, when the other man was about a yard away, Panshin let his foot slip.

The tray went up, and the soup and bowls came down—all over Marcel, who gasped both from being covered in hot soup and indignant shock at Panshin's clumsiness. Of course, Panshin was all apologies as he dabbed at the sodden tuxedo jacket while the other man cursed at him. Around them, servers continued coming and going, the flow of the kitchen not stopped for an instant while the two men tried to clean up.

"What has happened?" Henri was there in a flash, shaking his head at Marcel's soaked condition. "There is no time for blame now, we will sort it out later. Marcel, go and change. Yves, you will have to serve the president's table—and for God's sake, do not spill it on him!"

"Of course not, sir." Making sure he hadn't been splashed by any of the flying soup, Panshin headed back for the next tray of bowls, carefully picked it up and headed for the exit, making sure to avoid the large puddle already being wiped up by the cleaning staff.

Once inside the elevator, Panshin breathed a sigh of relief as his hand went into a pocket and separated the hidden lining to retrieve the small poison vial. Carefully—for he still had the tray balanced on his shoulder and hand—he unscrewed the cap with his fingers, brought up the container and poured half into the bowl of soup he would serve to the president. Just a few drops would be enough, but he kept some in reserve, in case his target didn't eat the soup, or it spilled before reaching him.

The elevator dinged, and Panshin just managed to drop the vial into his pocket before the doors slid open, and he walked out into the hall, crossing to the dining hall, where he met his assistant.

"Where's Marcel?" the young man, Claude, asked.

"Got soup spilled on him," Panshin answered without stopping. "You and I are serving the head table tonight. Follow me."

Claude fell in behind him without question, and the

two men headed to the table on the right of the lectern, where the Austrian president was seated. The French president and his wife were also there, along with the minister of the interior and his spouse. On the way, Panshin quickly swept the room and saw the black-haired man on the perimeter of the room. He glanced at the table where Nejem and Darsi were seated, and got acknowledging nods from each of them—they'd spotted him, and would run any interference necessary. He was free to proceed.

At the head table, he stopped at a respectful distance and handed off the tray to Claude, then took the poisoned soup and served it from the left, as he'd been trained to do. "First course, cream of chanterelle soup, sir."

Knowing the president wouldn't start until the rest of the table had been served, Panshin quickly presented the other guests with the course. Trying not to appear too interested, he stepped back and surveyed the table, gratified to see that everyone was enjoying their soup.

With a signal to Claude, they started back to the kitchen. The poison would take effect in about five minutes—more than enough time to effect his escape. And if he needed another distraction, there was always Nejem and Darsi, although he would hate exposing them if he didn't have to.

Panshin glanced around for the black-haired man, but couldn't spot him without being too obvious about it. Instead, he kept moving, focusing on the doorway.

He had just reached the exit when he heard a slight cough from the other side of the room, followed by another. Glancing back, he saw the Austrian president raise his napkin to his mouth. Could it be affecting him that quickly? he wondered, since one of the symptoms was a dry cough. The president took another spoonful, and Panshin turned back and kept walking out, secure that the plan was coming off flawlessly.

BOLAN FINISHED HIS SWEEP as the soup course was served. He noticed the dark-haired server they'd seen in the kitchen was also the one serving the president's table. He touched the earpiece in his other ear, using it to contact Deschaines, still overseeing things in the security center. "Anything unusual happen in the last few minutes?" he asked.

"Only if you count an entire tray of soup getting spilled on a server," the man replied. "They had to switch out the man for the lead table."

"And replaced him with… Yves, was it?" Bolan asked with a slight frown.

"Yes, that's correct. Why?"

"I'm watching him work right now, that's all." Bolan began heading back toward the president's table, watching for any sort of disturbance or commotion, but all seemed to be well.

The pair of servers finished attending the table and began heading back toward the entrance. Just then Bolan's phone vibrated.

"Go," Bolan said.

"Striker, this is Stony Base. Be advised, a man named Yves Montauk was found dead in his apartment an hour ago, his throat crushed. He was a server for the Hôtel de Marigny."

"I just saw the guy walk out the exit! I'm on him. If you're inside their security system, alert the command room and stay on him." Bolan was already moving toward the doors, scanning for Palomer. Spotting her finish her sweep, he trotted over to intercept her.

"The Austrian president's probably been poisoned—most likely something in his soup," he said, even as he heard a cough from the far side of the room. "The server who just left is an impostor. I'm going after him. Contact Deschaines, fill him in and get the president to a hospital right now!"

Bolan whirled on his heel and started for the door, only to hear a commotion from the far left side of the room.

"Please, give her some room, she's choking!" One of the journalists was trying to help his female partner, who was clutching her throat and turning red. Bolan trusted that the interior security could handle it, and left it to them.

He had just reached the door when there was a shout, followed by several rapid gunshots. Drawing his own pistol, Bolan turned just in time to see the reporter standing over a downed security man and aiming a pistol straight at him.

9

The room erupted in chaos at the first shots, with men and women leaping from their chairs and starting to rush toward the exit. The rest of the security personnel drew their weapons but hesitated, unable to get a clear shot on the attacker in the stampede of guests.

Bolan barely had time to register all that as he dived to the side, hitting the floor and coming up on the far side of the doors. Bullets whizzed by, drilling into the far wall.

Screams and shouts could be heard from the panicked mob now, but they were avoiding the exit after seeing the young woman firing at the doors. Bolan rose to his knees, then peeked around the edge of the door frame and nearly took a bullet for his trouble.

The two Al-Jazeera reporters had turned their table on its side and were using it as cover. The man had now gotten a pistol from another downed guard, and was busy fending off the other security forces. The guests huddled against the walls, protected to some degree by the remaining security officers.

"Cooper, get the other one!" Palomer shouted from the far side of the room as she laid down a burst of fire from her pistol. "We'll get these two!"

But even as she said that, the man broke from cover and ran toward the group of terrified guests, who screamed and cowered as he approached. One of the nearby guards opened fire, but the man ran through the hail of bullets, even though he had to have been hit by at least one round, firing back until one of his own shots dropped the French officer.

He grabbed an older woman by the arm and hauled her to her feet. "No one moves, or she dies!" Curling his arm around her throat, he held his pistol to her head while dragging her back toward the barricade the woman was hiding behind.

"We're leaving right now!" he said to the room. "If anyone tries to stop us, this woman gets shot!"

Forcing her to move with them, the two began shuffling toward the door, the female reporter right behind them, watching his back. At that moment, several things happened.

The woman, at least in her sixties, clutched her chest, gasped, "My heart!" and went limp in the man's arms, drawing his attention down to her.

At the same time, Palomer, who had been using the right side of the tables as cover to approach the shooters's position, aimed her pistol at the female reporter and squeezed the trigger, even as Bolan took the opportunity to aim at the man's exposed upper chest.

The hostage-taker was already looking back up at the door when Bolan fired three times. The bullets took him across the collarbones and breastbone, dropping him to the floor, the woman spilling from his arms.

Simultaneously, his backup grabbed the bottom edge

of the long dining table with one hand and flipped it up into the air and straight at Palomer. The sergeant barely had time to dodge out of the way as the spinning furniture flew past her to smash into the lectern and dais.

"Come on!" In the time it took for the table to hit the floor, the female reporter had reached the side of her fallen partner, who had gotten back up, bleeding, but still very much a threat. The pair ran for the door, their pistols blazing.

Bolan tried to return fire, but the fusillade of bullets was too much for him, and he had to take cover behind one of the columns in the reception room. When her pistol ran dry, the female reporter didn't stop running, she just kept sprinting for the stairway that led to the main doors, with her companion covering their retreat. For someone who Bolan knew he'd put three bullets into, the guy was moving like he was barely hurt.

What the hell's up with these two? he thought. Giving chase, he was at the stairs when he heard a shout from behind him. "Cooper!"

He turned to see Palomer burst into the room. "Get the Rover and get out front!" he shouted back. "Find me—I'll be chasing them!"

"Right!" She headed toward the back as he ran to the exit, only to see bright lights outside, and suddenly hear more gunfire.

A bullet punched through the heavy door as Bolan approached, making him duck to the side. He reloaded his pistol, wishing he had something heavier, then was about to contact Tokaido when he heard the clomp of many shoes running across the reception room's marble floor.

"Deschaines?" he called out. "Don't shoot. It's me, Agent Cooper."

"I hear you, Cooper, hold on." Moments later, Deschaines, followed by four security men wearing bullet-proof vests and carrying HK MP5s, was on the entry landing with him. "I thought you and Sergeant Palomer came here by yourselves."

Bolan frowned. "We did."

"So the shooters outside *aren't* yours?" the head of security asked.

"No, I'm trying to figure out what the hell's going on out there, as well."

"Apparently a third party is on the scene—but for whose side? They appear to be taking on the two there, but our reinforcements are still three minutes away." He nodded back toward the hall. "What happened in there? It got crowded when the woman opened fire."

"There were three assassins—a server, and a two-person backup team posing as reporters," Bolan replied. "They got to the president with poison, but I'm pretty sure he got evacuated."

At the other man's nod, he continued. "The primary's in the wind, and the secondary team took a hostage to make their escape. She collapsed, and I shot the guy holding her, but they kept going and got to the main entrance. I was about to pursue, and here we are."

"Right. Well, if we can catch them in a cross fire, we might be able to take them down," Deschaines said.

"Maybe, or they'll both turn on your people." Bolan eyed the subguns. "I don't suppose you have a spare?"

Deschaines shook his head. "Sorry, can't help you. We do have extra SIG Sauer magazines if you'd need them." He held out two.

"Yes, thanks." Bolan tucked them into his pockets.

"All right, guys, we need to take down both groups,

or at least hold them here until reinforcements arrive," Deschaines said. "Team One, you're on the hall shooters. Team Two, you engage the newcomers. Let's see if we can take at least one of each alive. Hit the door in three-second increments. Let us lead, Agent Cooper. You'll come out with me at the end."

He waved the first pair of his body-armored men forward. They took positions on either side of the door, then with a nod at each other, shoved it open and left the building. After a few seconds, the second two-man team went out, followed by Bolan and Deschaines.

The outside of the Hôtel de Marigny looked like a warzone as the two shooters exchanged fire with a team in the lot that had taken cover behind nearby limousines and the building itself.

When the French security arrived on the scene, there was a brief moment of confusion as the local men yelled at both groups to lay down their weapons and surrender. As Bolan had expected, both groups immediately turned and began firing on the French.

"Mon Dieu!" Deschaines shook his head as he ducked behind one of the columns. "We have to keep them here!"

"That's going to be harder than you might think," Bolan said.

With a flurry of fire from the second group keeping their enemies' heads down, the hall shooters broke and ran for a nearby limousine. "Of course the vehicle is facing away! We can't hit the engine!" Deschaines said as the limo came to life and roared out of the driveway. "We have to go after them!"

As soon as the car left, the other team began to back, scattered shots keeping the French security force at bay as they withdrew.

"So, they're not after us, but want the others, too," Deschaines said as he pulled out his phone. "I'm bringing our cars around. You're welcome to ride along with us—"

A horn blared from the road, and Bolan looked up to see Marie Palomer behind the wheel of the Range Rover. "Are we following or what?" she called to him.

"Thanks, Deschaines," Bolan said, "but I've got a ride. Catch up with us when you can." He bolted down the steps and over to the SUV, diving into the rear driver's-side door. "Go, go, go!"

Palomer gunned the V8 engine, and the big vehicle shot forward into traffic. "Let me guess," she said as he scrambled into the front seat. "We're following the speeding limousine."

Bolan checked the load on his SIG Sauer, then rolled down his window. "No, we're *stopping* the speeding limousine."

"How are you doing?" Amani Nejem didn't look back as she pushed the ponderous limo faster through the evening traffic.

"Fine. The subcutaneous skinweave stopped the bullets with minimal damage. I'll be sore, but it's better than the alternative," Kisu Darsi replied. "How's your head?"

"It is all right," Nejem lied. One of the outside group's bullets had creased her scalp, leaving an ugly furrow and making her bleed like a stuck pig. Her hair was matted and sticky, and blood had dried in a mask over half of her face. She was sure she didn't have a fracture, but her vision had been blurry for a couple of minutes, and even now her head was pounding from the near miss.

"We'll have to clean you up as soon as we can stop,"

Darsi mused as he checked his pistol's load. "I'm almost out of bullets."

"And I am out." She nodded at the empty pistol in her lap, the slide locked back.

"Get on the Champs-Élysées. There's more room to maneuver, and a better chance to lose them in traffic."

"I know where to go, thank you. I actually lived in Paris for a year, remember?" Nejem replied. She turned off the Avenue de Marigny onto the broad main avenue, merging with the evening traffic with minimum trouble, even though she was still going fifteen miles over the posted speed limit. "Keep watching behind us for anyone following."

"Yes, yes. So far, so good." Darsi was silent for a moment. "Do you think those other operatives were from the motherland?"

"I know they were," Nejem replied. "They picked us up more quickly than I had expected. I thought we'd have another day or so before they caught up."

"Staying in Paris this long is what allowed it," Darsi said. "We should have left after the US senator hit."

A job you should have finished properly, she thought, but didn't say. "Have you tried calling Alexei yet?"

"I left a message saying we got out—" Darsi slapped at his pocket. "That's him. Hang on, I'll put him on speaker."

He answered the phone. "Where are you?"

At the same time, headlights appeared in the limo's rearview mirror. "I think we have company," Nejem said.

"I'm in our car, heading west on the Champs," Panshin said. "Where are you?"

"Just turned on the avenue ourselves, now passing Avenue Montaigne," Darsi said. "There's another group after us—not the French. Amani thinks they're from home."

"That was to be expected in time."

"Well, they're gaining on us right now," Nejem said.

"Excellent. Just keep them on you for a couple more minutes," Panshin said. "I'll come up behind them and give them a surprise they won't forget."

"Whatever you plan to do, do it fast," Nejem said. "They are not in a mood to take prisoners."

"I'll be there in ninety seconds," Panshin said before he cut the call.

"It's going to be a long minute and a half," Darsi said.

"Well, make yourself useful and look around back there. There must be something you can use as a weapon."

"Already on it," he said above the clink of glass. Nejem looked in the rearview and saw him smiling at her. When she looked down long enough to see what he was working on, she smiled, too.

SERGEI BERSHOV, THE TEAM'S stolid bruiser and wheelman, was driving the Mercedes-Benz SUV, guiding it behind the limo with deft flicks of the wheel. Mikhail Sevaron was in the passenger seat, reloading his weapons and Bershov's. Natalya Zimin and Illya Krivov were both in the back, ready for the second round.

"Any signs of pursuit from the hotel?" Sevaron asked.

"No, which is strange," Zimin replied. "By now I would have thought we'd have a small army on us after a shoot-out this close to the palace."

"Most likely they'll be tracking us with helicopters,"

Bershov grunted. "They're probably already setting up a roadblock as we speak."

"All the better to take out these two now, and get out of here," Sevaron said, his eyes glued to the approaching limo. Just a few more yards…

"I thought for sure that head shot would have taken the bitch out," Krivov said as he chambered a round in his HK pistol. "If they can withstand this ammo at that close range, we're going to have to get really lucky to get a killing shot on them."

"It can be done," Sevaron assured him. "A concentrated assault will put enough lead into them that something vital will be hit."

"We are close enough now, if you want to try to stop the car," Bershov said.

"Yes, an accident would work well." Sevaron rolled down his window. "The car overturns, they are injured or stunned, and we turn around and take them out. Pull up alongside the driver's side. We can finish this in a few minutes."

Bershov tromped on the accelerator, and the powerful SUV began gaining on the limousine. They had to cut around a Peugeot in the lane Sevaron wanted, and for a moment he was tempted to have Bershov tap the guy's bumper, but kept his mouth shut.

Spotting them, the limo cut across two other lanes as they entered a large roundabout, cutting off cars with a screech of brakes and blare of horns. The SUV followed, nimbly avoiding the stopped traffic and steadily gaining on the limo until it was in position.

Sevaron readied his pistol and aimed at the front tire. One shot would be all it took.

"Look out!" Krivov shouted from the backseat as he opened fire with his gun.

The team leader glanced up to see a figure standing in the open sunroof of the limo, a flaming bottle in each hand.

"WHAT THE HELL was *that*?" Palomer demanded as a burst of flame bloomed near the SUV as it pulled alongside the limousine. The fire pooled on the road, already burning out, and she swerved to avoid it.

"Molotov cocktail," Bolan replied. "After the firefight outside the Marigny, they're probably low on ammo, so they're improvising weapons."

Another bright flare of fire licked at the SUV, this time staying on the side of the vehicle before the rushing wind blew it out. Both shooters on the passenger side returned fire, pocking the limo's side with holes.

"Ah, there's backup," Palomer said with a smile as two marked police cars, lights flashing and sirens wailing, appeared in the distance behind them. "I'm sure more will be behind them, as well."

"Good. With this new team in play, we're going to need all the backup we can get to take them all down." Bolan glanced behind them in time to see one of the police cars spin wildly and plow into another car beside it.

The second police car slowed to check on the first, allowing a black SUV with tinted windows to pull up alongside of it. A burst of flame erupted from the driver's window, and the hood of the second car leaped into the air as its engine failed.

"Damn—so much for our backup," he said.

"What?" Palomer checked the rearview. "What happened?"

"Near as I can tell, the primary assassin just showed up, and *he's* trailing *us*," Bolan said. "We've got hostiles in front *and* behind us!"

"Now what do we do?" Palomer asked.

"You stay on the two vehicles ahead of us," Bolan said as he began crawling into the rear cargo area. "I'm going to keep the assassin behind us from catching up to his two buddies. Get ready to lower the back window on my mark."

10

Steering with his knees while speeding along at almost seventy-five miles per hour, Panshin nimbly reloaded his compact SR-2 Veresk submachine gun while catching up to his team. With the two police cars out of the way, he expected to have smooth sailing to come up behind and catch the Russian team unaware. By then it would be too late.

The drivers of the nearby traffic seemed to have gotten the idea that something odd was happening, for some of the cars were moving to the outside lanes. However, there was still more than one vehicle content to trundle along in the middle of the street, blocking his way. *Typical SUV,* he thought as the temptation to give it the same tap he'd given the police vehicle rose within him, but he resisted, instead pulling out on the driver's side, simply intending to pass the slower driver.

That was when the rear door's window slid down, and a man's arm came out holding a pistol.

Although the shooter started firing as soon as he was lined up, starring the windshield, the Russian operative still had enough time to jerk the wheel hard over—not away, but toward the enemy vehicle. His turn sent the heavy SUV into the back end of his target, the front and rear quarter panels scraping together under the impact.

With his other hand, Panshin returned fire, blasting out the rest of the ruined windshield as he raked the other vehicle with a hail of thirty 9 mm bullets. Windows shattered and pebbles of safety glass sprayed across the road.

The other driver finally wrenched the SUV away from him, and it slewed across two lanes, nearly clipping the curb, and making pedestrians scatter for cover. Panshin stayed on it, ejecting the empty magazine from his subgun and reloading. The other driver had regained control, and headed back out into the middle of the wide boulevard. Panshin pursued, more cautious now, as he didn't know whether he had taken out the rear gunner. Three flashes of flame and bullets hitting his vehicle let him know he hadn't.

At least, not yet. He smiled while leveling his weapon at the tailgate of the SUV, intending to fire as many bullets as it took to eliminate the shooter.

About to squeeze the trigger, he heard the ululating scream of more French police vehicles approaching, and glanced behind him to see a pair of motorcycles speeding through traffic toward him.

Panshin calmly aimed and fired at the vehicle ahead, even as the shooter popped up and fired several rounds, this time aimed at his SUV's engine.

Slugs drilled into the Range Rover's rear door, and he knew at least one of them had to have penetrated—the only question was had it penetrated the shooter?

Even as he tried to see, a gout of white smoke or steam—Panshin wasn't sure which—burst from under the hood of his vehicle, which lurched and began to slow, shuddering as it lost power. Red warning lights bloomed on the dashboard, and the steering wheel felt sluggish under his hands.

As it rolled to a stop in the middle of the lane, traffic flowing around it, Panshin saw the two police officers pull to a stop several yards behind him.

"Throw out your weapons and come out with your hands up!" one of the officers commanded, first in French, then in English, his pistol aimed at the driver's window.

Glancing at the full duffel bag on the passenger seat beside him, Panshin smiled as he reached for the door handle.

"THAT'S THE LAST ONE!" Darsi shouted as he hurled the flaming bottle at the still-pursuing SUV. This one glanced off the hood but didn't shatter, arcing high into the air to come down well behind it and turning the street into a pool of fire that made oncoming cars screech to a halt.

"At least it's a diversion for anyone behind them," Nejem said as she whipped back and forth, trying to get some distance between them and their pursuers. "Where the hell is Alexei?"

"Maybe he ran into other police?" Darsi called from his vantage point poking up out of the roof. "Or perhaps that dark-haired man?"

"Regardless, we can't keep this up much longer. If they get within range, we'll be shot to pieces."

"I'm open to suggestions!" Darsi said.

"Well, first we'll try to lose them in traffic," Nejem said as she cut across two lanes of traffic, the long limo sideswiping a Renault sedan, which honked furiously as she turned left onto the Rue Quentin-Bauchart, a one-way street. "You might want to come back inside."

"You're going *where*?" Darsi asked as he dropped into the rear passenger area in time to see the blindingly bright headlights of oncoming traffic heading straight for them.

The next two blocks and fifty-eight seconds were among the most harrowing of Nejem's and Darsi's lives. Not even shooting their way out of the Hôtel de Marigny could compare to avoiding the cars, trucks and panel vans clogging the street, often by just a layer or two of paint. Once, when both lanes were blocked, Nejem screeched to a halt just enough so she wouldn't crash into a Lexus in front of her. However, she didn't stop either, smacking into the luxury sedan hard enough to shove it out of the way with a long, ugly dent and scrape down its passenger side. Gunning the engine again, she forced her way through the narrow opening, losing both side mirrors in the process.

"They're still behind us," Darsi said. "I could take a shot—"

"Save your bullets. We may need them later," Nejem said through clenched teeth as she spun the steering wheel back and forth, only her superior eye-hand coordination and razor-honed reflexes preventing them from piling up on more than one occasion. "Let Alexei know we're going to ground!"

Finally, they were through, and burst onto the short portion of Rue François 1er before hitting the T-intersection where it met with the Avenue George V. Hauling hard left on the wheel, Nejem bashed her way through nearby traffic waiting to merge and turned left again, heading toward the Seine. Their destination was less than a half mile away now.

"Almost time for us to ditch this car," she said to Darsi. "Grab the gear and get ready for a swim."

"What gear?" he asked even as the SUV, which had had an easier time following in their wake, tried pulling alongside again. Nejem drifted left to stop them, but it had been a feint, and they swung wide right and tried to pull up.

She corrected with a vengeance, smashing the limo into the side of the SUV and rocking it over onto its left tires for a moment. The impact rebounded her car to the other side of the road, and for a moment she faced oncoming traffic again before getting back into her own lane.

They had just passed the Rue de la Trémoille when the SUV caught up with them again. This time it stayed back, and the two shooters on the passenger side began trying to take out the rear driver's-side tire. After several shots, one of them hit, and the tire blew out with a bang.

The limo slowed, but Nejem kept the gas pedal crushed to the floor, urging the crippled car to keep moving forward. She could see the lights of the Pont de l'Alma in the distance, but first she had to navigate the busy intersection of several main thoroughfares that met right before it.

Leaning on the horn, Nejem shot the wobbling limo into the intersection, with the SUV hard on its tail. Cars screeched to a halt and rear-ended one another as their drivers tried to avoid hitting the speeding black car, only to end up getting nailed themselves by other drivers.

They had just reached the Cours Albert 1er when it happened. A car had just started to pull out, and Nejem couldn't avoid hitting it. She did manage to jerk the wheel to the left just enough to avoid a head-on collision, but the right front corner of the limo exploded in a crumpled spray of plastic and glass as its head- and turning lights disintegrated in the impact.

The other car spun out of the way, and she goosed the faltering car onto the bridge. "Ready?"

"Yes," he replied as he buckled his seat belt. "But I think you might want—"

His words came too late. The moment she was sure they were over the water, Nejem cranked the wheel hard right. The limo jumped the curb, blowing out both tires in the process, and leaped awkwardly into the air, smashing through the glass-and-metal guardrail and plunging toward the dark water several yards below.

It would have hit the surface, if there hadn't been a sightseeing boat approaching the bridge at that exact moment. Falling like a three-tonne rock, the limo punched through the boat's fiberglass-and-wood prow, and continued on its way into the river, leaving the panicked tourists and crew to abandon ship as best they could.

Once the car was completely submerged, Nejem and Darsi freed themselves from their seat belts and maneuvered through the open windows, swimming underwater until they were several hundred yards downstream of the accident. Finding a deserted dock, they hauled themselves out of the water and began walking away.

"Damn it!" Mikhail Sevaron smacked the SUV's roof in frustration.

With all eyes on the accident in the Seine, the Russian cleanup team had taken the opportunity to leave the scene before they were spotted. However, Sevaron wanted to keep an eye on what was happening with the car, so they drove to the next bridge and parked by the side of the Cours Albert 1er.

Using binoculars, they watched the efforts of the

French police, river patrol and other boats as they rescued the soggy passengers from the sunken boat. A crowd had gathered to rubberneck, and sometimes the Russian team could barely see over them. With Sevaron standing on the running board of the vehicle, he looked just like any other nearby gawker.

"Any sign of either of them?" Natalya Zimin asked.

From inside the SUV, Sergei Bershov shook his head. "They won't be here anyway."

Sevaron blew out an exasperated breath. "He's right. They've escaped by now and could be anywhere along the river."

"You don't think they could still be in the car?" Illya Krivov asked.

"If you want, you can hang around until they raise it and find out," Sevaron said as he turned on his heel and stalked back to their SUV. "But I'll bet you a year's salary it's empty."

"You pick up anything yet?" he asked the big man, who had an earpiece in his ear to listen to the police frequencies.

He nodded. "A motorist shot two police officers and stole a bike. Last spotted heading west on the Champs-Élysées."

"Let's go. I'll drive." Sevaron closed the passenger door and ran around to the driver's side.

"If he's on a motorcycle, we'll never catch up to him," Krivov pointed out.

"We're already in too deep over this whole mess, and we're still the closest we've been to them since getting here," Sevaron said as he swung into the driver's seat. "We're going to keep following them until either they or we drop, and it better be them first."

Starting the engine, he leaned on the horn until the

small crowd that had gathered even this far away slowly parted. "God save me from people with nothing to do," Sevaron grumbled as he eased the SUV through to clear road. "Guide me, Sergei."

"Well, right now they're on back on the Champs-Élysées," Bershov said, showing him a possible route. "If you take these roads, we might be able to come out just behind them."

Sevaron's only reply was to stomp on the gas pedal, making the SUV rocket forward onto the street.

11

"Where are they?" Palomer asked as they drove farther down the boulevard. "It's like both vehicles just up and disappeared."

"Get on the radio and see what you can find out," Bolan said, still watching behind them. If the police took that assassin into custody, he'd want to talk to the man before he went to trial.

From the front, he heard Palomer talking in rapid-fire French. Bolan took the time to contact Akira Tokaido at the Farm.

"I need eyes on the Champs-Élysées," Bolan said, "looking for two people in a limousine heading west-northwest, followed by four in an SUV. Gunfire and improvised explosives were exchanged between the two vehicles."

"I've got a lot of commotion along the river," Tokaido replied, "but not too much on the road— Wait a minute… I've got someone coming up behind you at a high rate of speed."

"What? Where?" Bolan stared down the long, straight

avenue, but there were too many lights from oncoming cars to pick out a single one easily.

"They're approximately five hundred yards out and closing rapidly. A limousine went into the Seine a few minutes ago, damaging a cruise boat as it did. Is that anything?" Tokaido asked.

"I don't know—hang on." Above the traffic noise, Bolan heard the high whine of a motorcycle. He thought he saw its headlight, but there were no sirens.

"How about a report of two police officers shot and a motorcycle stolen on the Champs-Élysées?"

"Damn it, that's the one! Stay on him, Akira! Marie, we're going to have company!" Bolan said, even as bullets chopped into the body of the SUV. A blur streaked by them, flame and slugs spitting from the submachine gun held by the driver.

Caught by surprise, Palomer hadn't gotten a chance to try to take him down with the vehicle. Instead, she'd hunched down as the assassin had shot by, then punched the gas again. "Damn it, he's not getting away from us!" she said as she pushed the SUV ahead ever faster.

But the man on the motorcycle was a veritable demon on two wheels. He shot through gaps Bolan thought he himself might have difficulty making, and in one instance used a Porsche 911 in the opposite lane as a ramp to clear a traffic snarl stretching across all eight lanes. Palomer lost precious seconds clearing the sidewalk so she could go around and resume the pursuit.

Despite how fast they seemed to be going, they hadn't gotten more than a few miles from the Hôtel de Marigny. She had radioed in their position, and sirens could be heard in the distance, but they were too far off to set up any sort of effective cordon or roadblock.

"I'm tracking him now—wait a sec," Tokaido said.

"He's slowing. He's stopping at the Arc de Triomphe… he's ditching the bike and heading into the Metro, Charles de Gaulle-Etoile station."

"Metro station at the Arc, hurry!" Bolan said. "Keep tracking him, Akira."

"I'm on him."

The giant marble arch was visible in the distance, but it still took an agonizing minute to get close enough to get out and continue on foot after radioing in their location. Bolan and Palomer ran though the arched corridor and down the stairs into the broad tunnel.

The platform was sparsely populated, with only a couple dozen people standing along the edge waiting for the next train. Trying to quiet his breathing, Bolan quickly scanned up and down the platform, looking for the dark-haired man without trying to look conspicuous. Even the lightly populated area could become a bloodbath if the man pulled his gun and began shooting again.

"I don't see him anywhere, do you?" Palomer asked.

"No. He must be hiding among these people. Let's head down to the end and take it all the way back."

Bolan hadn't gone more than a half dozen steps when he saw the man leaning against the wall near where the train would enter the station. He'd ditched his black tuxedo jacket, and had a duffel bag slung over his shoulder, hanging between his body and the wall as he stared at his phone, just like most of the passengers were.

"I've got him, six yards ahead, against the wall," he said quietly to Palomer. "I'm going to take him. Cover me."

She nodded, pulling her pistol and keeping it down at her side as she fell in a pace behind him.

Bolan kept moving forward, covering the distance between him and his target in three long strides. But when he unleathered his pistol, the man was already turning toward him, bag held at his side—with his other hand inside it.

In that moment, Bolan realized his mistake. "Yves" was going to shoot through it! The Executioner lashed out with his foot, connecting with the bag and shoving it up as the man pulled the trigger. The end of the duffel exploded in fire and lead, and the sustained chatter of the burst echoed loudly down the tunnel.

At the same time, Bolan pulled the trigger of his pistol, the bullet hitting the guy in the lower abdomen.

Screams erupted along the platform as people scrambled to get away from the shooter. Palomer shouted something, hopefully instructions for people to evacuate, but Bolan couldn't pay attention to that, as he had his hands full.

The man's phone hand shot out and slapped Bolan's pistol away, hard enough to throw off his balance for just a moment. His opponent's leg snapped out, and Bolan managed to pivot just enough to avoid taking the foot in his crotch. Instead, the blow landed on his thigh and was strong enough to make him stagger backward.

Shaking it off, the Executioner tried to bring his pistol back on line, but the guy was coming at him now, and he moved fast. Bolan thought he had a bead on him, but he dodged out of the way, and the next thing he knew, his adversary had grabbed his pistol and stripped the slide off with one hand, dropping the pieces to the ground.

Then the assassin stepped closer and aimed a palm heel strike to Bolan's nose. He barely dodged it, feeling the man's hand displace air as it grazed the side of his head, then he felt pain there, and realized the guy had turned his hand to gouge at his ear and cheek on the return.

Bolan had faced many opponents in his time, going up against every sort of combat expert in the world. His own style of fighting was swift and deadly, and rarely could anyone stand up to it for very long.

He grabbed the man's hand as he pulled it away, but his opponent freed it before he could get a solid grip. No matter. Still holding the bottom of his pistol, he threw it at the man's head, unsurprised to see him duck. That was unimportant, however, as it had only been a feint anyway.

Bolan stepped in and lashed out with another snap kick, this one aimed at the man's stomach. The simple, powerful blow often stopped a fight cold if executed correctly, and this one was a masterpiece, striking the other man squarely in the pit of his stomach—right where he'd shot the man, as well—and should have dropped him to the ground, puking his guts out.

That, however, didn't happen.

The first thing Bolan noticed was how solid the guy was. He might as well have been trying to kick a brick wall. Also, the guy *took* the shot, stepped back just a bit with the impact, then trapped Bolan's foot, obviously intending to pull him off his feet and slam him to the floor.

Instead, the Executioner launched himself into the air, intent on kicking the man in the face with his other foot while both hands were occupied. Stunned by the shot to the face, the man would release his foot, and Bolan would be able to pull at least one of them back to land. It was a risky move, requiring incredible physical control and split-second timing that few martial artists in the world could pull off, but its surprise factor guaranteed that no one would be able to stop it.

This man, however, did. He got a hand free and up to intercept the blow before it connected, pushing his attacking foot upward. With his other shoe still held firmly, Bolan crashed to the concrete platform, hard.

But the assassin wasn't done yet. Before Bolan could recover, the man twisted his opponent's foot, hard enough to make him flip over to avoid breaking his ankle. The only problem with that was that he was already on the edge of the platform, and now he went over, crashing onto the tracks a yard below.

The man jumped down behind him and took off into the dark tunnel.

"Are you all right, Agent Cooper?" Palomer asked from above.

"Yeah," Bolan said as he rose to his feet, even though he didn't feel all that great—not physically, but because he had underestimated his opponent. "Where's this tunnel lead?"

"Ternes station," she replied.

"Have all reinforcements converge there," he said over his shoulder as he ran into the darkness. "I'm going after him."

"Wait! I'm coming with you!"

"You can't!" he called back. "There's no cell phone reception down here. You have to stay and make the call!" After that, he didn't look back, concentrating instead on listening for the man's footsteps in the dark.

Bolan ran about one hundred yards up the tunnel, then slowed to a walk as he listened for sounds of the man's passage. His blood pounded in his ears, and he tasted copper from where he'd bitten his tongue when he landed on the Metro tracks.

That was when he realized he couldn't hear the man's footsteps anymore.

He was too far down for the light from the platform to do him any good. Slipping his hand into his pocket,

Bolan grabbed his smartphone and pulled it out just as he heard the scrape of a shoe on the ground.

He turned toward the noise just in time to get his jaw almost torn off by a powerful kick that made stars explode in his vision and sent him to his knees. Even so, he managed to lash out with a fist, but connected with nothing except air.

"You can't win, you know." The voice, light and mocking, echoed in the tunnel, seeming to come from all around him. "Who are you—an American? Are you the best they could send?"

Bolan gingerly touched his jaw, which bloomed in fresh pain at the merest pressure from his fingers. "Yeah, I am. Who are you?" he asked as he slowly rose to his feet again.

"I'm something you cannot even begin to comprehend." Shoes scraped over gravel again, and then another heavy blow struck Bolan, this one on his calf, causing a blinding pain that nearly paralyzed his lower leg. "I'm the next generation of warrior, far superior to you and your obsolete kind."

In the distance, the far-off rumble of an approaching train echoed down the tunnel, and a glimmer of light pierced the darkness from around the bend.

"In fact, since you're so obsolete—" A hammerblow pounded Bolan's kidney, numbing the entire lower half of his back and sending him to his knees. He fired an elbow at where he thought the guy should have been, but again his strike found only air, and he nearly toppled from being overbalanced.

"—I think it fitting that you die right here." The assassin hadn't moved as far away now, and Bolan seized the slim opportunity. Raising his smartphone, he triggered its camera, which also set off the auto flash.

As he'd hoped, the bright light in the man's face blinded him, and he staggered backward.

The light from the train now illuminated the tunnel, and Bolan saw the man's silhouette a few yards away. He charged forward, intending to tackle him and bring him to the ground, but just as he was about to get his hands on him, the man spun aside as he brought his fist down on the back of Bolan's head, driving him to the ground, stunned.

The assassin bent and flipped him over onto the tracks, staring into his face. "You will never find us. You will never stop us." Then he took off again, sprinting toward the oncoming train.

Bolan tried to push himself up, tried to crawl over to the narrow space next to the tracks, but his arms and legs refused to obey his commands. The train's headlight was blinding now, overwhelming his vision, the thunder of its approach drowning out everything.

His last thought before the blackness took him was that this was not how he'd expected to die…

12

"Agent Cooper? Agent Cooper!"

The insistent voice, along with a sharp, acrid smell wafting under his nose, conspired to jerk Bolan back to consciousness. He blinked and threw a hand up to shield his eyes from the bright lights of the Metro station. Blurry, indistinct shapes drifted around him, resolving into Palomer's worried face, and the face of a paramedic.

Looking around, Bolan saw he was lying on the concrete platform near the train tunnel, and that all of his limbs were intact. "I'm surprised that I'm in one piece," he said.

"You can thank her for that," the paramedic said with a nod at Palomer. "She went into the tunnel, found you and moved you into a maintenance recess in the wall, then carried you out here. She saved your life."

"Thanks, Marie," Bolan said as he attempted to sit up, wincing as more stars went supernova in his head. Nausea clenched both his gut and his brain, and he leaned over, breathing shallowly through his mouth until the feeling passed.

The paramedic started to repack her bag. "We need to take you to a hospital to get a look at your head. You've taken some nasty blows—I'm frankly amazed that your jaw isn't broken—and the fact that you lost consciousness is a concern."

"I appreciate the offer, but I can't spare the time." Slowly, he turned his head to look at Palomer. "I don't suppose they caught our guy at the next station?"

She shook her head. "DGSI closed it as soon as they got word, suspended all trains on the line and sent in a special tactics squad to sweep the entire tunnel, but they found nothing. There are several places where he could have gotten out by using maintenance tunnels or access to the sewers. He's gone."

"But definitely not forgotten," Bolan said. "We've got him and the other two on camera, and you and I both got a look at his face. We can cover the city with a BOLO announcement, and hope we get lucky…" His head throbbed again, and a gray fog clouded the edges of his vision. "You know, while we get those stills made from the hotel security cameras, maybe I should get checked out. It just can't take very long."

Palomer nodded. "Good, and don't worry. We'll take you to the American Hospital of Paris. Since it's private, the doctors should be able to expedite any tests they want to run. We can make some calls on the way and get the photo selection started. Now, come on." She indicated a portable, wheeled gurney brought in by the paramedics. "Let's get you out of here."

"Thanks, but I can walk."

"Who's coming out?" Illya Krivov asked from the backseat.

"Not anyone we're looking for..." Mikhail Sevaron said as he watched the Metro entrance through binoculars. "Unless...perhaps there is a way to use all of this craziness to our advantage."

"How so?" Natalya Zimin asked.

"Take a look at the tall man with black hair walking to the ambulance," Sevaron said as he passed the binoculars to her.

She raised them to her eyes, then lowered them. "He was at the hotel."

"He's American, and from what I've been hearing from DGSI radio transmissions, it sounds like he and a companion either foiled the assassins, or disrupted their plans at the very least. I think he's after the same thing we are—stopping the products of Utkin's program."

"And perhaps more," Zimin said. "What if the Americans have gotten wind of Utkin's program and want to capitalize on it? Then they wouldn't be content with just stopping these operatives."

"They'd want to capture them if possible, or at the very least, take one of the bodies with them for autopsy," Sevaron finished. "Good thinking, Natalya."

"So, how do we proceed?" Krivov asked.

"I would like to know what they know if possible, so I think a more direct approach is in order," Sevaron replied. "Sergei, let's head to the embassy. We'll need some new identification papers. Make sure you know what hospital he's taken to."

"And let's also requisition some armor-piercing bullets," Krivov said. "Although I'm not surprised HQ sent us insufficient equipment, I am surprised it was *this* insufficient."

Sevaron nodded. "It will be done."

"What is the plan?" Bershov asked.

"Natalya and I will make contact, posing as FSB agents on the trail of the assassins, and offer to join forces with the American," Sevaron said. "Sergei and Illya, you will be our shadows, ready to back us up if necessary, and also, when the time is right—" he grinned mirthlessly "—we will destroy the assassins *and* eliminate the American in the interest of national security."

THREE HOURS LATER, Mack Bolan lay on a bed in the American Hospital of Paris, feeling a lot better. He'd gone through a complete CAT scan, and although the doctors were concerned about the large bruise he had on the back of his head, they said there appeared to be no visible damage to his brain, although they wanted to keep him overnight for observation, which he was strongly resisting.

In the meantime, Marie Palomer and he had turned his room into a makeshift command center. On the way over, she had called Alain Deschaines regarding the photos from the camera footage, only to find he had already organized a collection of the best shots, and he emailed them to her. Bolan had been in contact with Akira Tokaido for the same thing from his button camera. By this time, they had excellent shots of all three available.

"Of course, this assumes that they weren't wearing any sorts of disguises," Palomer said as they readied the best pictures to be made into BOLO announcements that would be distributed not only across France, but to Interpol to pass along to intelligence agencies across Europe and North America.

"True, but even if they change their appearance, putting the word out about them should make them more wary about continuing their operations," Bolan said, even as the assassin's words echoed in his head. *You will never find us. You will never stop us…*

"Yes… I just hope they don't go to ground or flee the city," Palomer said. "This is a calculated risk we're taking to go public with an act of terrorism."

"We have no choice," Bolan reminded her. "With seventy witnesses to the attempted assassination, followed by a high-speed chase and firefight on the main thoroughfare of the city, I think a lot of people are already aware of what's gone down. Also, was anything discovered at the apartment of the real Yves Montauk?"

"After everything that's happened, I almost forgot about that poor man." Palomer checked her phone, then shook her head. "Nothing out of the ordinary. He was apparently selected due to his position at the hotel, and his resemblance to the assassin. There's nothing else linking them."

She sank into a chair and sighed. "It is always a cat-and-mouse game with these terrorists. We make one move, they make another. Sometimes I don't see how we'll ever win against them."

"First, don't forget that despite all the damage and destruction, you and your people didn't fail. The Austrian president survived." The latest update they'd received was that he was in serious but stable condition, undergoing chemical detoxification to neutralize the poison in his system.

"That is true, but it came at a high cost," she said. The final tally was five of the hotel security killed and two wounded, along with the two motorcycle officers shot and killed on the Champs-Élysées. The press was already screaming about it in their overnight editions, and the television news shows were merciless in their condemnation of the national security forces.

"Every one of those men and women understood that they may be called on to lay down their lives for their people and their country, and they did so without hesitation, just as you would, I'm sure," Bolan said. "The fact that they helped save the president makes them heroes. That's cold comfort right now, but their sacrifice still means something.

"Finally, it helps to take the long view about this fight," he said. "Sometimes it's a gain of inches instead of yards or miles. For me, every day I'm still breathing to oppose them is one more day of fighting the good fight. Every one of these jackals I take down is one more that won't be around to spread their terror anymore. These three are just another bunch on the list, that's all."

"Except they're not just your everyday run-of-the-mill terrorists, are they?" Palomer asked. "I know what I saw, both at the hotel and in the Metro station—they were able to shrug off bullets like they were nothing. I *watched* you shoot that man at point-blank range, and he didn't stop."

"High-level body armors can stop a bullet, even at close range," Bolan pointed out.

"Maybe so, but did it look like he was wearing a bulletproof vest?" Palomer asked, shaking her head. "You and I have both worn them and seen others wear them. We know what they look like. That guy wasn't wearing one." She blew out a breath. "Plus, he moved like no one I'd ever seen before. Watching the two of you fight. You're obviously no slouch, but I'm sorry, you weren't in the same league as him."

Bolan acknowledged that the guy had hit like a jackhammer. Everyone examining him had sucked in their breath when they saw the large bruises on his jaw, lower back and leg. Even he wasn't sure how he hadn't dislocated or broken his jaw from that first shot to the face.

"You may be right, but I've got something none of them have—experience," he replied, filling her in on his smartphone distraction. "Trust me, our next meeting will be quite different."

"I hope so—for all our sakes," Palomer replied, biting her lower lip. "There's also another element I'm concerned about with all of this."

"Yes," Bolan asked as he gingerly adjusted his position on the bed. "Thanks to your file on the previous events that these killers are tied to, there is a pattern emerging here, besides the obvious tie of striking against anyone who speaks out against Russia. Their targets are escalating in terms of power, as well."

She handed the list of the incidents to Bolan, who scanned them, and nodded. "You're right. So, who would be next? The UK prime minister? The US President?"

"It would probably be best to see what international events are occurring in the next few days, and who's attending," Palomer said. "Off the cuff, my guess would be that they'd want to strike something much like what they found here, only on a larger scale, perhaps with two of their perceived enemies on-site."

"Right. I'll get my people on it." Bolan had filled her in on his connection with "his" people, although he'd been deliberately vague about any details, and now he contacted the Farm.

"Striker to Stony Base."

"Striker, this is Stony Base," the gravelly voice of Aaron "the Bear" Kurtzman rumbled in his ear. "Go ahead."

Bolan filled him in on his conversation with Palomer regarding future targets.

"Striker, we'll prepare a list immediately. Were there any parameters you want us to use to narrow it down?"

"The best I can think of would be to focus on Europe and North America, although I'd think flying would be a major issue for them at this point, especially once we get the BOLO out. Let's stick with Europe, including the United Kingdom for right now. If nothing actionable comes up, we can expand outward."

"Roger that. As soon as we've finished crunching the data, I'll be in touch."

"Got it. Thanks, Bear." Bolan disconnected the call and leaned back again, strongly considering trying to grab a couple hours of rest. A knock on the door interrupted that notion, however.

Palomer was already on her feet and heading to the door. She cracked it open. "Yes?" Muttered voices could be heard outside, and she leaned back a bit. "Just a moment."

She turned to him. "Two FSB officers are outside, requesting to see you."

Bolan raised an eyebrow. "Now *that* I did not expect." He thought for a moment, then shrugged. "Have them come in—might as well see what they have to say."

The moment Palomer turned back to the door, Bolan subvocalized to Kurtzman, "I think I'm about to have a very interesting conversation that you're going to want to hear."

"Understood, Striker, my ears are on," the computer expert replied. "Let's see what the Russians have to say about all this, shall we?"

13

The second-story flat in the red-tiled house on the outskirts of Paris was located in an unremarkable neighborhood where students and young people often found more affordable housing that was still within commuting distance of the city.

Shrouded in an oversize hoodie he'd purchased from a street vendor, Alexei Panshin arrived at the house at 0135, having walked the 11 miles from the middle of the city. After the debacle in the Metro, he didn't trust any form of transportation that might have a camera, a human operator, or both, so he'd come back to their secondary safehouse on foot. The walk wasn't difficult—he'd endured marches ten times that length during training.

He stood on the other side of the street and checked the windows. A small lamp with a blue shade was on in the upper right corner, meaning all was clear. Checking both ways on the street, even at that hour, Panshin crossed and let himself in the side door, creeping up the stairs so as not to awaken their landlord.

Amani Nejem and Kisu Darsi were already at the house, and had changed their appearances to more easily escape the country. Nejem was now a striking blonde, with light hazel eyes. It was a stunning combination against her dusky skin. Darsi had shaved his beard, and was in the process of wrapping a turban around his head. They both tensed when he slipped inside, with Darsi holding a pistol out of sight behind his leg. They relaxed slightly when he pushed back the hood.

"You're sure you weren't followed?" Nejem asked as she crossed to the window and looked out over the deserted street.

"Trust me, no one could have followed me considering the route that I took," Panshin said. "Are you both ready to go?"

"Just about," Darsi said, tucking away the end of his turban. "You are aware that we failed in our mission here?"

Panshin scowled. "I had heard on the way over." Indeed, he'd weighed the possibility of trying to find the president and finish the job, but had realized it would be impossible to improvise that with the heavy security around the man. "Nothing can be done about that now. We must move on."

"The plan is still the same, correct?" Nejem asked.

"Yes, the final target will make landfall in Madrid in less than twenty-four hours. We will be on the road within the next sixty minutes, and will be there in plenty of time to set up, including placing the explosives. How is my skin tone looking?"

"You're already at least two shades lighter," Nejem said, examining Panshin under the light. "I still cannot believe the skin changer actually works so well on you—it's incredible. Are you dyeing your hair here?"

"I'd better," he replied. "The sooner all of us are altered, the better. I think I'm going to try the freckles, as well. Once you're both done, make sure everything is cleared out of here."

"What about...?" Darsi pointed at the floor.

"Let me finish up here first, just in case, then you can go prepare everything for our exit."

Forty-five minutes later, Panshin had wavy ginger hair instead of the black, and his skin tone was nearly pale, with a light smattering of freckles dusting his cheeks and nose. Combined with light blue contacts, he looked nothing like the man who had been at the Hôtel de Marigny earlier that evening.

At last, they were ready to go. Panshin sent Darsi to the ground floor to eliminate their landlord, a kindly old lady. Once that was done, they got into their car, a nondescript Kia sedan, and drove off.

"I AM OFFICER Mikhail Rosnovich, and this is my partner, Officer Natalya Kepar," the Russian agent said, offering his hand, which Bolan took. His grip was firm, callused and dry. His face was affable, but none of that expression came close to his eyes. He spoke excellent English. "We understand there was a bit of excitement here earlier this evening."

"Depends on what you call 'excitement,' I suppose," Bolan replied after introducing himself and Palomer.

"Well, I would say slain police officers, public shootouts in the street and an attempt on the life of the visiting Austrian president is plenty of excitement, wouldn't you?"

"Why don't we get to the reason you're both here?" Palomer asked.

"Ah, direct—I like that," Rosnovich said, looking

around. "Do you mind if we sit down? This story may take a while."

"Sure." Palomer rose from her chair. "Officer Kepar can have my seat."

Rosnovich had pulled the other one, near the door, closer to the bed. "Let's see, where to begin—"

"How about confirming that we're all after the same targets—three Russian assassins who are trying to take out high-level targets that hold anti-Russian views in Europe," Bolan suggested.

Rosnovich nodded. "*Da*, that is correct. However, I wish to be very clear about this. We, and by that I mean my government, did not sanction their actions, and we disavow any prior knowledge of their mission."

"Then who did?" Palomer asked.

"That is simple—Dr. Rostislav Utkin." Rosnovich offered to Bolan a picture of a slender, stoop-shouldered man with short gray hair and dark, probing eyes. The Executioner stared at it a moment, ensuring that the button camera he'd installed on his hospital bed got a good look at the face, then passed it to Palomer.

"All right, I'll bite. So how does a doctor unleash a wave of sophisticated killers on the continent?" Bolan asked.

"Dr. Utkin was no ordinary physician." Rosnovich leaned back in his chair. "This all goes back a couple of decades, and of course, much of it is classified state secrets. However, I will tell you what I can.

"Russia has many programs involving emerging technologies. We try to stay on the forefront of advances in medicine, health, the human body, et cetera.

"Around 1990, Dr. Utkin proposed a long-term study to create the perfect government operative. Utilizing infants that had no ties to country, family, or anything else in the world, he developed them into the perfect soldiers—enhanced, skilled, smart, chameleonlike, unquestioning of their superiors and very dangerous.

"Recently, our military was forced to cut its budget," Rosnovich continued. "Dr. Utkin's program was one of the ones on the chopping block. Although he appeared to take the news in stride, soon after he dropped out of sight, and then these…incidents began happening."

"So, he decided to show his superiors just how effective his soldiers could be in a real-world scenario," Palomer said. "In my country."

"Unfortunately, we would say yes, although yours has not been the only nation affected, if that lessens the blow a bit."

"It doesn't," she replied stiffly.

"Plus, I must say that from what we have been able to understand, your internal security forces acquitted themselves quite well."

Bolan glanced at Palomer in time to see her stiffen. "The families of those dead officers might disagree with you about that," she shot back. "And your so-called admiration does nothing to lessen this tragedy that was directly caused by your nation."

"Again, these operatives are carrying out their missions without my government's sanction. They are rogue, and therefore have been targeted by the FSB to be stopped by any means necessary."

"Officer Rosnovich—"

"Mikhail, please."

"Mikhail, all of the targets the assassins have struck at have shown a decided anti-Russian bias. I assume that is part of Utkin's mission that he assigned to these operatives."

The Russian agent shifted on his chair—a bit uneasily, Bolan thought. "Utkin is a party hard-liner, completely committed to Russia and the fallen Empire. He wishes to restore the motherland to its former glory... by whatever means necessary."

"Also, you said he 'developed' these operatives. How so?" Bolan asked.

"I'm afraid I cannot reveal too much of that. Again, state security prohibits me from doing so," Rosnovich replied. "What I can say is that they have been raised since birth to be the perfect tools of the state—no fear, no hesitation, no deviation. They are like homing missiles. Once they have locked on to a target, they will simply keep going at it until it or they no longer exist."

"And based on what we've experienced with them, they've also been physically modified as well, haven't they?" Bolan asked. "Perhaps some implanted body armor, maybe a ceramic skullcap? I think this Utkin also may have been experimenting with adrenal gland stimulation as well. Stop me if I'm too far off the mark."

Rosnovich smiled blandly. "Again, regrettably, I am not allowed to discuss the details of the program. What I am here for is to offer our assistance with stopping these combat machines before more people are killed."

"You'd like to join forces?" Palomer asked, her eyebrows lifting in disbelief. "May I ask where your people were in the previous twenty-four to thirty-six hours, when receiving this information during that time might have saved lives?"

Rosnovich spread his hands. "Unfortunately, the information we had on these operatives, including their appearance, was out of date. It seems that Utkin might have had some sort of forewarning about his program ending, and modified his most recent reports accordingly. Therefore sending you incomplete information would have been as bad or worse than sending none at all. We had to wait for them to make their move before we could reveal our own presence."

"Of course—hoping that you could take them out before we could," Palomer spit.

Rosnovich didn't offer a response to her challenge.

"Regardless, we appreciate your presence now," Bolan said. "Sergeant Palomer and I need a few minutes to discuss what you just told us, and it needs to be run through the proper channels. I'm sure you understand."

"Of course, of course. Just please let your people know that we stand ready to assist in any way possible," Rosnovich said as he and Natalya rose from their chairs and walked to the door. "We will be outside, awaiting your decision."

With that, they left, closing the door behind them. "Well, the more things change, the more they stay the same," Bolan said, leaning back and putting his hands behind his head.

Palomer didn't respond until the door clicked shut. The moment it did, she whirled to face him. "Surely you can't be serious about working with them?"

"As serious as getting my bell rung by that guy," he replied, waving her closer to the bed. "I know that doesn't sound like the most appealing option at the moment—"

"The most appealing option? It sounds like the worst one!"

"I understand that you're furious that they brought this to your country, inadvertent though it may have been. Wait a minute," he said as she opened her mouth. "It's true—these two aren't responsible for their government's choices, they just got assigned to clean up the mess. Besides, we also don't have much choice at the moment. If we say no, do you really think they're going to just pack up and go home? No chance. At least this way we can keep an eye on them, and who knows, perhaps get some more intelligence on these altered humans, or their scientist creator."

Palomer eyed him coldly. "And let me guess—the CIA wouldn't mind getting its hands on Utkin if the opportunity arose, right?"

"We can argue about that some other time," Bolan said. "I won't lie. If the orders come down for me to bring the guy in, that's what I'd try to do—emphasis on try. However, it sounds like he went deep into Russia somewhere, making it hard to find him, and even harder to get him out of wherever he is right now. First things first. We have to stop these three killing machines before they strike again, and my priority is to take them down, period. Not capture, not disable, but exterminate. If the Russians are our best bet to do that, then that's what we should go with. Agreed?"

The sergeant stared at him for a long moment, then slowly nodded. "Agreed. Although you've sure got a funny way of seeing things from their point of view… almost like you trust them."

"Funny," Bolan said with a wry grin, "I never said *anything* about trusting them. Look, you need to inform your superiors about this new wrinkle, and so do I. Why don't we do that and get our respective marching orders, and then we can regroup and figure out how to proceed from there, all right?"

"Yes, I should report in. No doubt Lambert's just waiting to ream me out for this."

"Hey." Bolan pointed a finger at her. "You did absolutely everything you could this evening, including saving my life. Nobody can fault you for your actions tonight, and if they try, you just let me talk to them, Lambert, your President, or whomever."

"Thank you, Agent Cooper," Palomer said.

"One more thing—call me Matt," Bolan replied.

Palomer nodded. "All right." She walked to the door. "I'll be back in a few minutes."

"I'm not going anywhere," he said.

"Bear, did you get all that?" Bolan asked as he adjusted his earbud, grateful for the hi-tech communication gear developed by Gadgets Schwarz.

"What's the plan, Striker?" Kurtzman asked.

"I'll tell you in a few seconds," Bolan replied quietly as he got up and walked to the two chairs the Russians had occupied. A quick search revealed the two tiny bugs each agent had placed on each chair. Bolan moved the chairs near the bathroom door, then turned on the tap full blast and walked back to his bed. "Sneaky FSB tried to bug my room."

"Just like old times, eh?" Kurtzman said. Bolan could hear the smile in his voice.

"Yeah. We should probably bring Hal in on this."

"I've got him holding on the other line. Hang on, and I'll patch him in."

"Striker," Hal Brognola said, "what in the hell's going on over there? I'm watching the French news blow up over this attempted assassination of the Austrian president, and the yahoos on the Hill are all running around like the sky is falling. And you are aware that the President is landing in Madrid for an international summit in less than six hours, right?"

Well, I think we know what their next target is going to be, Bolan thought.

"It's not quite that bad, Hal, but there's definitely some things that need attending to." He gave the big Fed a rundown of everything he'd done and learned in the past six hours, ending with his chat with the two FSB agents. "So, unless you say otherwise, I think I should team up with them and see where it all goes."

"With our luck, it'll be into a black box and then rendition to some bag site in Algeria," Brognola grumbled. "Still, the old adage of keeping friends close and enemies closer makes sense, I suppose."

"Of course it does," Kurtzman said. "Besides, if Striker turned the Russians loose, they'd still go after the targets anyway. They can't afford to have them fall into anyone else's hands. The fallout of possible illegal human modification would be catastrophic for the Kremlin."

"Bear brings up a good point," Bolan said. "Is it viable enough to try to bring in one of these subjects?"

"Only if you can do it without endangering yourself or others," Brognola replied. "And judging from what you've told us, that doesn't sound very feasible."

"Well, they're not going to defect willingly, that's for sure," Kurtzman said. "It might be better to just take them out cold, and then see if we can figure out a way to get at the scientist. He already burned his bridges with his government. It's highly unlikely they'd welcome back a loose cannon like him. An offer of asylum might just be the ticket out he's looking for."

"Possibly, but first things first, Bear," Brognola said. "Striker, you take care of business there, and then we'll figure out what to do about this toy soldier maker."

"All right, but these guys definitely aren't toys, and I've got the bruises to prove it. One more thing, Hal." Bolan paused. "Given the precarious state of affairs over here, wouldn't it be wiser if the President were to cancel his trip? That's a huge target, and one I'm almost certain these people are going to go for."

"Yeah, you try telling POTUS there's something he shouldn't do," Brognola groused. "No, it's still on, part of the whole 'we will not bow to foreign extremism' shtick they trot out every other year or so. There's a lot of people in Wonderland who have a huge interest in seeing the EU stick around, and they've been pushing hard for several weeks to make sure this trip happens, come hell or high water. Sometimes I think he's going just so they'll shut up about it.

"Bottom line—get these guys, protect the President and save the day, Striker."

"I hear ya. Striker out."

14

"I cannot hear anything." Natalya Zimin pressed on the earpiece harder, as if by shoving it into her ear she could magically hear the conversation going on in the next room. "Nothing but what sounds like static or running water."

Mikhail Sevaron's mouth creased into a knowing smile. "This Matthew Cooper does not trust us, eh? Well, I suppose it is to be expected. I wouldn't either, if I were in his shoes. Ah well, it is of no consequence. In fact, it is probably better that both sides understand they are using each other. It is so much better to work with professionals who understand the game play instead of amateurs."

"Speaking of amateurs." Zimin nodded at the young Frenchwoman striding down the hall toward them from wherever she had disappeared to—probably to consult with her superiors, as well. "Working with her over the next few days should be…interesting, to say the least."

"We will both be civil and professional until the job is completed. Then we will see how to handle both of them." Sevaron nodded pleasantly at the woman as she knocked on the room door, then let herself in.

Zimin waited until the door was closed before snorting quietly. "Any intelligence agency that gets into a scandal over improper editing of its entry in Wikipedia is amateur in my book."

Sevaron grinned. "Indeed." He stretched his arms above his head. "I would kill everyone within sight of us just for a halfway decent cup of tea right now."

The two operatives cooled their heels in the hallway for another minute before Palomer poked her head outside.

"We're ready for you now." She opened the door wider. "Please come in."

"Thank you, Sergeant Palomer." As Sevaron entered the room, he didn't hear any water running. He also noticed that their chairs had been moved next to the bathroom door. The man who had introduced himself as Matthew Cooper was now fully dressed and sat on the edge of the bed, watching them both.

Sevaron held his stare, but the black-haired man didn't give an inch. Quite the cool character, the Russian thought. We'll see just how cool he is at the end of all of this.

"Sergeant Palomer and I have been in touch with our respective superiors, and we would like to accept your offer of assistance in this matter."

At Sevaron's nod, Cooper continued. "Based on all available information, we are reasonably certain the assassins are headed for Madrid, and the international summit meeting of the European Union, where our President is the keynote speaker."

"Such a gathering of dignitaries, government officials and diplomats from around the world will be an irresistible target for them," Palomer added.

Sevaron nodded again. "That makes sense. With the summit beginning in less than twenty-four hours, we do not have much time. How would you advise that we proceed?"

"We have arranged for a jet at Charles de Gaulle, and ideally we should spend the time in the air figuring out a way to locate them before the summit begins," Palomer replied. "We have already alerted all law enforcement in the city, as well as the security of the visiting attendees, but with such a large contingent of people arriving over the next day and a half, it will be a very difficult task, particularly if the assassins altered their appearances since leaving the city."

"It's too bad your Dr. Utkin didn't include a tracking device on them when he was building these people," Cooper said.

"He was supposed to, but he either never activated it, or they rendered them inoperative themselves," Sevaron replied. "We will just have to use good old-fashioned legwork, deduction and intuition."

"Not to mention the resources of two of the largest nations in the world," Cooper said.

"Of course. If you are ready to go, we should really be on our way, as every second counts, correct?"

"That's right." Cooper rose off the bed and walked toward the door, with Palomer ahead of him. Together the four of them left the hospital and got into a waiting SUV driven by a DGSI officer.

As they pulled away, Sevaron subtly checked behind them to see the replacement SUV containing Sergei Bershov and Illya Krivov fall in behind them. Pulling out his phone, he texted that they needed to take the next available commercial flight to Madrid.

Then he settled back in the comfortable seat and re-laxed, prepared to let the American and the French-woman do all of the work, and allow them to swoop in and take care of the rogue assassins when the time came.

DRIVING STRAIGHT THROUGH the night at often dangerous speeds, the Russian assassins arrived in Madrid about an hour after dawn. The city was just starting to ramp up its day, and as they approached, the blend of various time periods, given Madrid's centuries-old existence, became more evident its architecture. The city had held on to a great deal of its history, seen primarily in the Spanish Golden Age structures of the sixteenth and sev-enteenth centuries, which emphasized austerity instead of flamboyance. Yet here and there were evidence of other styles as well, from the Middle Ages simplicity of the Bishop's Chapel to the Renaissance styling of the Convent of Las Descalzas Reales, with its simple exte-rior, looking more like a government building or even a prison, giving way to a beautiful church interior. Every so often more modern buildings jutted toward the sky.

Amani Nejem was particularly taken with the city as they drove in on the A2, looking at the massive Madrid-Barajas Airport as they drove past, and the large Prín-cipe Felipe Convention Center that would be their target in the next twenty-seven hours.

Driving past the center, they took note of the ongo-ing preparations, with rows of large trucks unloading tables and chairs, and catering trucks unloading food-stuffs and other supplies.

"This one is not going to be easy," Kisu Darsi mused as they passed the huge building. "Truly it's a pity the operation in Paris did not go as planned. Surely everyone will be on their highest alert here."

"That may be true, but it is of no matter," Nejem said. "This is the kind of thing the doctor created us for, trained us for. We have the skills to handle it, don't we, Alexei?"

Alexei Panshin glanced at her from the driver's seat. His freckles had appeared in full on his now pale skin, blooming across his face in small dots. "Of course we do. We are the wolves among the sheep. No matter how well protected they think they are, we will prevail. We are the harbingers of a new era for our country, never forget that."

They were staying at the Hotel Neuvo Boston, less than a mile from the center. It was also close to the airport, and they had already made plans to leave the city by plane if possible. Arriving without incident, they checked into their adjoining rooms, and met up once they were situated.

"The real question is whether our original plan is still viable," Darsi said. "We drew a lot of attention in Paris, and the American Secret Service are going to be very much on their guard."

"Not to mention those operatives who are no doubt still attempting to track us, whoever they might be," Nejem added.

"I have been considering both of those issues ever since we left the city," Panshin said. "Which is why I believe we need to alter the plan to distract at least some of our pursuers." He looked from Nejem to Darsi. "That is why I want you two to set a trap for the officials still chasing us. That should allow me to infiltrate the summit and complete our mission. Once that is done, we can then leave the city and move on to our next operation."

Nejem and Darsi exchanged a glance. "But, Alexei, the plan called for all three of us to prepare the auditorium. It was going to be quite a job for all of us, to say nothing about one person doing the setup."

Panshin nodded. "I know, and I've thought about that, as well. With the heightened security, one man executing our plan will draw less attention than three. And if the people back in Paris show up—as we all know they will—then we have to have a way to distract them. Having both of you appear in the city will at least force them to split their forces, or perhaps even draw off entirely and chase you, leaving me free to execute our plan."

The other two nodded. "That makes sense," Nejem said. "If we can stop the black-haired man from getting on-site, then that is one less obstacle you must worry about."

"Exactly. I know we do not have much time nor additional supplies, so I will leave the particulars up to you in terms of how you wish to entrap them. Just be sure that you do it far enough away that they are unable to get to the center in time tomorrow."

"Agreed." Nejem nudged Darsi. "Come on, we need to get out into the city so we can be seen."

"It's going to be a long day," Darsi grumbled as they both grabbed whatever gear would be suitable for their mission out of what was left and exited the hotel room.

Meanwhile, Panshin began preparing for his own mission, and his own long day that lay ahead—starting with infiltrating the convention center to begin his mission to kill the American President.

AKIRA TOKAIDO YAWNED so hard his jaw cracked. He rubbed his eyes. Ever since the Paris debacle, he'd been working the screens nonstop alongside Aaron Kurtzman, both men aggregating data and distilling it into their most accurate hypothesis about the assassins' next moves.

But even with the highest probability showing that the killers would go to Madrid to attack the EU summit attended by the President, that still left them with the problems of finding them and figuring out *how* they were going to attack.

Of course, if we find them before they can put their plan into motion, then that solves the second problem, he thought. Which still leaves the first problem...

Tokaido returned his attention to the hundreds of pictures flashing by on the large monitors before him, each one representing a camera feed in Madrid that Stony Man's computers were all observing, looking for any people who might resemble the assassins, and then following up with highly detailed scans and running facial-recognition programs to get a match. So far, the computers had isolated six people, but the scans and evaluations had all come up with very low probabilities on them, certainly nothing to raise an alert over. Tokaido had flagged them anyway, so the mainframe would continue tracking their movements, just in case they had somehow come up with a way to defeat some of the most sophisticated physical-analysis software in existence.

Another monitor was devoted solely to the people coming and going at the convention center. Between attendees, their security personnel, press and the center staff, there would be more than fifteen hundred people on-site for this conference. And every one of them was being scanned and filed in a huge database. Most would be eliminated immediately as people of interest, but with people constantly entering and leaving the sixteen-thousand-square-yard building, the list of scanned personnel was constantly changing every minute.

"And they said sitting at a desk for twelve hours a day wouldn't be exciting," the young hacker said to himself with a wry grin as the computer screen covering Madrid's bus services—all of which had had cameras installed a few years ago—flashed, indicating it had detected something of interest.

Tokaido looked at it and saw what appeared to be a cosmopolitan group of passengers heading into the heart of the city. The computer had flagged two people as persons of interest with an 82 percent match possibility, and he zoomed in on them and captured a still shot.

He moved the digital photo—which was decent, but not great—and ran it though the facial-analysis program. That came back with a 93 percent probability that these two were the backup team for the Paris assassin. The woman had dyed her hair and changed her eye color, but it still wasn't possible to alter the immutable contours of her face—cheekbones, skull measurements, orbital socket diameter—which was what the computer was comparing.

The man was even more obvious, clean-shaven, and with a turban covering his head and dressed in a white shirt, trousers and shoes. Both carried a pair of large shopping bags from a grocery/department store chain common in the country.

Tokaido checked the bus route. The vehicle was several miles away from the convention center, and heading farther from the site each minute.

What are they up to? he wondered. A secondary target? A diversion?

Whatever the answer was, he needed to let everyone know what was going on. Flagging it as a priority sighting alert, he sent it to Kurtzman, Brognola and Bolan, then returned to sifting through the raw feeds. Two had been spotted, which left one still out there…

"Hmm…" Mack Bolan tried not to frown as he studied the sighting alert that had just appeared on his phone screen.

The jet had gotten them to Madrid in just under two hours. Hal Brognola had notified the event organizers that four agents would arrive on-site to beef up security. They had immediately headed to the convention center, where they'd identified themselves to the security personnel and begun coordinating their perimeter setup. They took the time to review what the center already had in place to prevent a repeat of the Paris incident.

The head of security was a raven-haired woman named Genoveva Prieto, a consummate professional clad in a crisp charcoal-gray pantsuit. While she had welcomed them to both the city and the event, she had also made it clear that the city had final jurisdiction over any security procedures they wanted to implement, and that her people also had final say over any plans they wanted to enact. The Russians were reluctant to accept that, and only some smooth talking by both Bolan and Palomer had prevented an incident.

Now, he looked around to see the Russians reviewing a floor plan of the building and surrounding grounds, and Palomer sitting at a computer, checking over the attendee list. He walked over and bent to look over his shoulder as he placed his smartphone on the desk where she could see it.

"We've got a hit on the backup team in the city," he told her. "Let's keep it between ourselves for just a minute to work out how we want to respond."

Palomer studied the bus's route. "This is the AZCA financial district, and it's pretty far from the convention center. What's their goal? Are they going after a secondary target?"

"I have to think it's a gambit designed to lure us away from the primary," Bolan replied. "You'll notice that he's nowhere to be found, and we haven't picked up even a trace of him anywhere. They're trying to get us to split up our force, so he has a better chance of completing the mission."

"I agree, but what if they're actually going after a secondary target?" she asked. "They are in the financial district, and that makes sense. There are lots of people, and high-value opportunities for them. How do you want to play it?"

"Are you up for doing a bit of urban hunting?" Bolan asked. At her nod, he discreetly contacted Akira Tokaido. "Stony Base, this is Striker."

"Go ahead, Striker," the young hacker replied.

"Regarding that priority sighting you sent over, cross-reference the AZCA financial district with any companies there that might be anti-Russian in their trade dealings. Let me know if and when you find anything."

"Affirmative, Striker."

Bolan straightened and turned to the Russians. "Mikhail, Natalya, we have a sighting."

The two FSB officers joined him, and Bolan filled them in on what Stony Man had given him. They agreed with his assessment. "So, how should we handle this?" Rosnovich asked.

Bolan had already been wrestling with that. "Normally I'd suggest splitting up our team, since we really should have eyes on the primary target," he said. "However—and I do not mean any offense to anyone here—

I'm concerned that a two-on-two matchup against these two may be too dangerous to risk."

That, and I really don't trust you guys in this scenario, he thought. No one had mentioned the Russian president's notable absence from the summit—in fact, there was barely a Russian delegation at all, with just the country's ambassadors from Germany and Italy attending.

"Agreed," Rosnovich said. "At the same time, we cannot discount the possibility that they are planning another strike, and leaving it up to local officials would be like sending a trussed-up pig into the slaughterhouse—they would not stand a chance." He rubbed his chin. "It would appear that we have no choice."

For a moment, the four exchanged wary glances.

"Not particularly," Palomer said. "So we should get down there and stop them right now."

A knock at the suite door made everyone's head turn. "I'll get it," Bolan said, already walking to the door. A suited man stood outside, carrying a small, nondescript box that looked heavy. He walked in and set it on a nearby table, then held out a smartphone to Bolan. He pressed his thumb on the screen, then held the device up to his eye for a moment, waiting as it flashed. He handed it back to the man, who checked something on the screen, nodded, then left, closing the door behind him.

"What was all that about?"

"I had something delivered to even the odds for us," Bolan said as he opened the box. Inside were neatly packed boxes of ammunition, all labeled VBR-Belgium, with a bright yellow stripe around each. "We've got 9 mm, .40 caliber and .45 caliber, just in case."

Opening one of the boxes of ammunition, he held

up a round, which had a cone-shaped bullet that narrowed to a small point. "These armor-piercing rounds have the standard conical profile, and utilize a 6.3 mm hardened steel penetrator, allowing for a larger wound cavity. Most importantly, they can be fired from regular handguns, without any modification. As they've been proven effective against Level II and IIIA vests, I would think we should see similar penetration on whatever's inside the assassins." Bolan stared at the two Russians. "Unless you'd like to let us know if I'm wrong."

Rosnovich picked up one of the oddly shaped bullets. "I believe these should work," he stated.

"No submachine guns, I see," Kepar said.

Bolan shook his head. "Given the crowded environment we're entering, we think it's best to stick with pistols, to minimize the chance of a round hitting any bystanders."

Rosnovich nodded even as he appropriated an entire box of 9 mm ammunition. "Just in case," he said.

They took a few minutes to replace the ammunition in their magazines, then headed out in search of their prey.

15

Thirty minutes after Amani Nejem and Kisu Darsi left the hotel, Samantha George, aka Alexei Panshin, wearing a black silk turtleneck, matching slacks and black flats, long red hair pulled back in a clean ponytail, walked out of the elevator and out the main entrance. He got into a plain blue Renault sedan and drove the short distance to the convention center, where he went through two layers of security, including ID check and photo confirmation, as well as a complete car search, inside and out, including a bomb-sniffing dog check, just to enter the grounds.

He was stopped again upon entering the building, where his ID was checked once again. This time he was scanned with a metal detector wand and endured a physical pat down by a female security officer behind a screen. He submitted to all of it with patient good humor, even kidding with the woman assigned to him about her job. No one detected a man posing as a woman.

Once cleared, he was issued an on-site badge that would allow him strict access to only the areas of the building he was supposed to be in. Fortunately for him—primarily because his cover identity had been created for this exact occasion—that included the auditorium where the US President would make his speech the next morning. Although it would be tight, there was still enough time to prepare for his arrival.

Panshin entered the main lobby, which was a scene of organized chaos. Men and women walked or ran everywhere, putting the final touches on a gathering of the world's leaders that happened only once every several years. Various security details, their weapons often in plain view, coordinated with one another, as well as inspecting and overseeing installation of decorations and any additional equipment needed. They could be an issue, but Panshin was pretty sure he could handle any barrier they might throw at him.

He walked straight for the entrance to the auditorium, listening for anyone talking about the Paris incident, but heard nothing. Apparently these people were all focused on the present instead of the past—even the recent past.

At the door, both his badge and ID were checked yet again. They clearly weren't taking any chances. Panshin waited while the security man ran the final check, and then entered the room.

The large chamber could seat up to three hundred easily. It was vaguely bowl-shaped, with terraces for the audience so they could all see the speaker at the bottom of the room. A black iron grid of lights was barely visible in the shadows of the ceiling.

He asked for the operations supervisor, and was directed to a harried-looking man who was still impeccably dressed. He was surrounded by three people, each demanding his attention. He handled each issue with polite alacrity, then turned to Panshin. "Yes?"

He held out his hand. "Samantha George. I'm here to take care of the lighting for tomorrow's event."

He shook "her" hand once even as he pulled out a computer tablet and began scrolling through it. "George… George… George… Ah, here we are. So, you're one of the new additions to our family here. Welcome, welcome. I'm Javier Toset, general operations manager for the center. To be honest, we didn't expect you to come in until this evening."

Panshin smiled. "I prefer to familiarize myself with the setup and board well ahead of time, in the event of any issues that might arise."

"Smart thinking." He looked around. "Did you bring any gear in with you?"

"I believe my supply truck is out back in the loading area," he replied.

Toset scrolled some more. "Um…yes, it arrived this morning. We had it parked off to the side, due to the larger trucks coming in after it. I hope that won't be an issue."

"Not at all. As long as I have access to carts and electronic lifts, I think I'll be fine."

"All right, then, I'll leave you to it. The sound room is up there." He pointed to the wall of windows high up at the back of the room. "And access to the staging area is through the doors at the front of the room. Also, the room coordinator is Sara Alves, in the yellow blouse on the far side of the room. See her if you need anything. Otherwise, again, welcome aboard."

"Thank you, I look forward to working with you and everyone here," Panshin said with a smile. "Now, if you'll excuse me, I have plenty to do, as no doubt you do, as well."

Despite being distracted already, Toset managed to

return a game smile. "You have no idea. Good luck," he said before turning on his heel and trotting off.

Panshin headed toward the set of double doors at the back of the room, pushing through them to find himself in a stark, concrete loading dock that spanned the entire rear of the building. Here again, trucks were backed up to loading docks, unloading food, furniture, equipment and other items.

He walked by the bustling, straining, shouting men running back and forth to the far end of the loading area, where there was a door to the outside of the building. Locating an empty dolly, he grabbed it and pulled it behind him while stepping through the door. He scanned the crowded lot until he located the small white panel truck parked off to the side, almost like an afterthought.

Walking to the back of it, he consulted his phone and punched in the twelve-digit code that changed hourly on the keypad. The light next to it changed from red to green. If he'd entered the wrong code, the truck would have exploded. Opening the rear door, he stepped inside, hauling the dolly in after him.

The interior looked like a standard light rigger's van, with frames, lights, bulbs, gels and other tools of the trade on shelves and in cabinets lining both walls. In the center of the cargo area were two large black plastic boxes labeled Light Board Sensors—Fragile—Handle With Care.

Panshin keyed in a second code on the first of these boxes, which was booby-trapped similarly to the truck, and opened it to reveal a series of plain black ceramic cubes set in gray foam rubber cutouts, about four inches on a side. Small recessed arrows detectable by touch alone marked one side, indicating which one should be placed toward what the demolition person wanted to destroy.

If anyone asked him what the cubes were, he would say they were wireless sensors to monitor the status of the lights. There were maybe two or three people on the center's staff who might question that answer, and he doubted they'd even be bothering him as long as he looked like he knew what he was doing, and kept working. As with most places, fitting in was 90 percent of any infiltration job.

In reality, there was enough Semtex in one of these cubes to level a two-story house, and it was completely sealed from detection by chemical sniffers or bomb dogs. With the dozen cubes Panshin planned to place at key points around the roof, the resulting blast—timed by a mechanical timer to fire the detonator, so no wireless signals or electronics to disable—should be more than enough to bring the whole roof down on not only the American President, but the audience, as well.

The resulting deaths, ideally including several heads of state from various countries, should throw the EU into chaos, to say nothing of the death of the sitting US President. Amid all of the strife, it would be foolish for Russia to not move to consolidate some of the countries it had lost in the breakup of the USSR. At the very least, the resulting elections might enable more pro-Russian candidates to emerge on ballots and possibly get elected, smoothing the way for future relations and improved trade.

No matter what the results, this action would shake up the European Union, reminding it that it was still vulnerable, that just because the countries had joined together didn't mean they were more secure. It would also put the fear of Russia back into Europe, rather than the current state of affairs, where the nation was still seen as a crippled bear, hobbled by falling oil prices, rampant corruption and weak infrastructure.

Well, after today, they won't think we are so weak anymore, he thought. And if they wish to exact revenge for this action, they will soon find out that our claws are still as sharp as ever.

Another foam cutout contained a flat, narrow box that was also protected from X-rays and other detection methods, appearing to be simply electronic components when scanned. Panshin opened it and removed the compact, matte-black PSS pistol, designed for reconnaissance and assassination. Unlike sound-suppressed weapons, which only muffled each shot and still created noise, the PSS was a truly silent weapon, as each round of the special ammunition it used contained its own internal piston and propelling charge that fired the bullet. After the bullet left the chamber, the piston also sealed the neck of the cartridge, preventing any noise, smoke or flame from escaping the barrel, as well. Although its range was most effective out to twenty-five yards, it was still a nearly perfect weapon for a silent kill.

Panshin checked the pistol's action, then loaded it with 7.62 mm ammo and used a miniclip holster to conceal it at the small of his back. He slipped another full magazine into his pocket, loaded one of the boxes full of cubes onto the dolly and began hauling it back into the center. He still had a lot of work to do before the President's speech—his final one.

"YOU'RE COMING UP on them now," Akira Tokaido said. "Just another half block to go. They're sitting on opposite sides of the small plaza in the middle of that cluster of buildings on your left."

Bolan pulled to the side of the busy avenue and looked out his side window. The plaza was a flagstone-paved space about twenty yards on a side. A small fountain in the middle burbled into the air, the water glistening as it caught the sunlight. Modern stone benches were scattered around the area, many next to large, raised concrete platforms containing colorful flowers or small trees, lending a touch of greenery and shade to the area.

"Great. There's open ground, yet plenty of cover, and lots of people walking around. It's the perfect place to set off explosives or open fire on bystanders," Palomer said.

"Also plenty of places to run inside for more cover and hostages, as well," Rosnovich remarked. "If we're not careful, we could have a slaughter in several places here."

"I suppose calling in a bomb threat wouldn't help the situation any—you know, to evacuate the innocent," Kepar offered.

"Normally that might be an option, except they'd either lose themselves in the evacuating crowd or open fire on it, and we'd be screwed ether way," Bolan said. "If they're still there, waiting for us to arrive, we need to figure out a way to take them here and now, ideally without firing a shot."

"I don't see how that's going to be possible," Palomer said as she leaned forward to study the area. "They got looks at all of us back in Paris, so we can't approach them without tipping them off."

"Right, so we'll just have to figure out another way."

He contacted Stony Man. "Akira, any change in either of them since they arrived here?"

"The only thing that's changed is that they are not carrying their bags anymore. Repeat, they do not have the shopping bags they entered the plaza with, but have placed them in or near the various trash receptacles around the plaza."

"Okay, but they did have them when they arrived?"

"Affirmative."

"Given the location they've chosen, I think the odds are very good that the bags contain improvised explosives that they planted," Rosnovich said.

"Clever. Do we try to apprehend them, or find and neutralize the bombs?" Palomer asked.

"We did tell you they were good," Rosnovich said from the backseat.

Bolan was quiet for a few minutes. "Akira, have you had eyes on the secondary team since when you first spotted them?"

"More or less, Striker, given what cameras I could find along their path," the Stony Man hacker replied. "The Spanish financial folks do love to keep an eye on their buildings, however, so I'd estimate I've had overwatch on them 90 to 95 percent of the time."

"Good. So if we have to call in a bomb threat on those shopping bags, you can provide the exact locations?"

"That is affirmative."

"All right."

Bolan turned to Rosnovich. "My guy said he can give the locations of where the bombs are," Bolan told the others.

"Akira, send me a top-down view of the plaza and the location of each target."

"Coming up." A few moments later, Bolan's smartphone chimed and he swiped at it to reveal the picture. Linking to the SUV's onboard dash display, he put the picture up for all of them to see.

"They're not taking any chances," Bolan pointed out. "Each one is situated so they can watch at least two entry points. The moment either one sees any of us, they'll draw and start shooting, not to mention probably set off one or more of the IEDs. So how are we going to take them both down with a minimum of casualties?"

Everyone fell quiet, thinking about the obstacles hampering their mission. "What we really need is a way to get close to at least one of them, preferably both, but I'd take one…" Palomer scanned the plaza again, then looked up and down the street. Her eyes widened, and she pointed down at the next block.

"There—that's our way in."

16

Ten minutes later, Bolan shuffled toward the plaza, staring at the ground, occasionally muttering to himself. He now wore a stained, filthy, olive green overcoat and dirty striped pants with a large hole torn in the knee, along with ragged, falling-apart shoes, one of which was missing its heel. The stiff breeze ruffled his already mussed hair. Everything he wore stank, and the people around him gave him a wide berth as he approached.

They'd bought the disguise for one hundred euros from a homeless man Palomer had spotted, and gave him Bolan's spare clean clothes so he wouldn't get arrested for running around in his underwear.

There'd been a brief but intense argument over who was going to actually wear the disguise, but Bolan had overruled Rosnovich by the simple expedient of grabbing the clothes and putting them on. Then there had been another brief discussion about letting him go in alone, but he had quashed that too by saying the last thing they'd expect would be to see just one of them.

As final touches, Bolan had mussed up his hair,

rubbed dirt all over his face and hands and put on a pair of sunglasses he'd gotten from Rosnovich. He ambled into the plaza, rattling a stained coffee cup to beg for change.

"So far, so good, Striker. They don't seem to be taking any real notice of you," Tokaido reported in his ear. "Just keep heading straight, and you'll be able to see the man on your left, in about four yards."

Palomer was on the sidewalk between the SUV and the plaza, pretending to talk quietly into her phone. In reality, she was connected to Bolan's phone, and was hearing everything he was doing. The Russians were positioned near one of the other skyscrapers, using the foliage in the planters to get as close as they could to the woman without being seen. When the operation began, they'd be able to get on-site in about five seconds. It would be a long five seconds, however.

Throwing his arm out like he was warding off an invisible assailant, Bolan next tucked it under his open jacket, as if he was scratching his stomach. In reality, he was making sure his pistol was easily available in his waistband.

"All right, he should be visible out of the corner of your eye. Do you see him?" Tokaido asked.

Bolan looked over to see a turbaned man sitting on the stone bench, leaning back against the stone planter, arms outstretched to either side. He casually watched people go by, although Bolan would have bet he was aware of everyone in the area, and was evaluating their potential threat level. Ideally, the Executioner would be seen as just another homeless person in the city, and therefore be overlooked.

Just as Palomer's plan intended.

"I'm going to take him," Bolan subvocalized to the others through his phone. "My shout will be the signal."

"Ready," Palomer replied.

"We're ready here," Rosnovich replied.

As SEVARON WAITED for the go signal, Zimin was on the phone to their backup team, which had been tailing them from the moment they'd left the convention center.

"Be ready," she said. "Be advised, the trash containers may contain IEDs. Approach with caution."

"Understood," Krivov replied. "We're in position."

Depending on how the American's initial takedown went, the plan, Sevaron knew, was that he and Zimin were either going to cut off the female assassin's escape, or reinforce the American if the male assassin proved to be too strong for him. With her fluency in Spanish, Palomer was supposed to handle crowd control, leaving the two Russians as the backup. In the chaos that was sure to follow, if they saw a shot to take down both the operative and the American, any of the Russians were supposed to take it.

Realizing Sevaron was looking at her questioningly, Zimin nodded at him.

"We're ready here," he said into his phone, hand on the gun hidden under his jacket, fully loaded with the armor-piercing bullets the American agent had supplied.

Zimin grinned as she readied her own pistol. The irony of the American being killed by the bullets he'd supplied was delicious.

She only hoped she would be the one who got to pull the trigger on him...

BOLAN'S GENERAL PLAN had been to get as close as he could to the man, then draw his pistol and try to cover him at gunpoint, taking him alive if possible. He was fully prepared to put as many rounds as he needed into the operative if necessary, however.

With the turbaned Russian only a few yards away, Bolan swayed on his feet, then staggered over to the corner of the large, square planter like he was going to throw up into it.

"He's ignoring you, Striker," Tokaido said. "He even slid down to the far end of the bench."

From his vantage point, Bolan could now get a good look at his target as he dry-heaved into the bushes. The turbaned man glanced in his direction once, then looked back toward the other side of the plaza. The time was now—

"Oh, shit, Striker, look out!" Tokaido said just as a heavy hand landed on his shoulder.

Although Bolan's first instinct would have been to spin, grab the offending hand and break either it, the arm, or both in one of six different ways, he remained in character and straightened as he was whirled to face a uniformed police officer.

The man spoke to him in a burst of rapid-fire Spanish, then grabbed Bolan by the arm and began pulling him toward the street, obviously intending to eject him from the space.

Bolan was in an even worse bind now. Taking down the cop would draw attention to himself, and possibly spook the two operatives, but if he allowed himself to be taken away, reappearing in the plaza again would be suspicious no matter what. And there was no way he'd be able to convince the policeman he was an undercover US agent, even with his credentials. He couldn't risk the man saying something that might be overheard by Bolan's target.

Shaking his head and mumbling, Bolan planted his feet, hoping Palomer was hearing what was happening and would try to intercede, even if it meant blowing her cover.

"Oficial, perdón, oficial," a voice said in perfect Spanish.

Bolan glanced up to see that Palomer had also transformed herself somehow. She now wore designer sunglasses and a large hat worn on the side of her head that hid her face when she stood next to someone. She trotted up, careful to keep the hat between her and the Russians. "Thank you for your assistance," she continued, her tone a mixture of relief and exasperation. "This man is my uncle. He has chosen to live on the streets, and will not come home with us, no matter how I beg him to. I have been waiting for him here, and now you have found him, which I appreciate so much."

"This man is your uncle?" the officer asked in Spanish.

"Yes. He is not well—mentally, you know," she replied. "I think we should go now, but again, thank you for your help, Officer. I am so grateful."

Taking Bolan's arm, Palomer began leading him out of the plaza. Bolan was thinking they were about to get away with it when the simplest thing happened.

A gust of wind spun up and blew the hat off Palomer's head before she could catch it.

Bolan glanced back, as if checking on the cop, but in reality he was checking on the turbaned man, who had been watching them. His eyes widened in surprise.

We're blown! flashed through Bolan's mind, and he whirled to leap at the cop, shouting, *"Pistola, pistola, pistola!"*

He had just gotten his hands on the man's shoulders

and was driving him down behind the planter when the turbaned man grabbed a compact submachine gun from behind the bench and fired at them. Bullets tore through the air overhead, and into the nearby street, the very thing they were trying to avoid. Screams and shouts erupted all around them as people scrambled for cover throughout the plaza.

The confused policeman went down underneath Bolan, struggling to draw his own pistol as he fought and kicked to free himself. Grabbing the other man's wrist, the Executioner scrambled to pull out his own identification before he got shot. He managed to free his ID and thrust it in front of the man's face before he could draw. *"¡Americano! Americano agente!"* he shouted. *"¡Pedir refuerzos!"* he said, ordering the other man to call for backup.

Even more confused now, the policeman stared at the ID while more shots rang out, this time from behind Bolan. The Executioner glanced over to see Palomer returning fire, one arm hanging uselessly at her side. "You okay?" he shouted.

She just nodded while continuing to put rounds near the shooter. "Just get him!"

The local cop had finally gotten the picture and shouted into his radio, presumably for reinforcements. He had also drawn his pistol, and Bolan left him there and began crawling around the other side of the planter, intending to catch the turbaned shooter from behind while Palomer kept him occupied.

He had just reached the far side when slugs whined off the corner he was behind, chipping off pieces of concrete and spraying them into his face. Bolan reared back, spitting out concrete dust and looking for the second shooter.

But these rounds were coming from the far side of the plaza, where neither of the Russians were located. "Akira, we've got new shooters. Who are those guys?"

"I was just about to let you know. Intel says there were four shooters outside the Hôtel de Marigny in Paris—these two are the rest of the Russian team!"

Mikhail and Natalya had backup there the entire time—and didn't tell them! Bolan thought.

He looked around for the other two Russian agents, but they were nowhere to be seen. It was possible that they were pulling a double cross, especially if the Russians wanted to make sure there were no witnesses to the cleanup of their loose cannons.

But judging by the fire coming from the other side of this planter, Bolan still had a larger problem to worry about—stopping the turbaned man before he turned the plaza red with the blood of innocent bystanders.

But before he could take any action against either shooter, a bright flash and a deafening roar, followed by a column of smoke and ball of fire, erupted from the far side of the plaza.

THE MOMENT THE homeless man had been accosted by the cop, Nejem had sensed something wasn't right. She tried getting Darsi's attention, but he was busy watching his surroundings while keeping watch over the situation next to him out of the corner of his eye.

She shot him a quick text warning him to stay alert, then glanced around, spotting a young woman sitting on a bench nearby reading from a tablet, with a baby stroller next to her. Nejem put a smile on her face and walked over to her. "My, what a cute baby!" she said in Spanish.

"Oh, thank you—" Distracted by the sudden compliment, the woman looked up just in time to see Nejem's pistol pointed directly at her face. The joy on her face was replaced by confusion at first, then fear.

"Uh-uh. Just keep smiling, and you and your baby will live through this," Nejem said, her own broad smile never wavering. "Listen to me very carefully, and do exactly what I say. Put the tablet away, pick up your bag, and then we're going to walk in the direction I tell you to go. Keep smiling, and act like we're old friends meeting up. Let's go now."

Her hands trembling, the woman managed to jam her tablet into her bag and pick it up, slinging it over her shoulder. Under the guise of helping her, Nejem moved to her far side, keeping the woman between her and the rest of the plaza. "Take the stroller and move, right now, walking normally."

"Just don't hurt my daughter," the woman begged.

"Do as I say, and she will be unharmed," Nejem replied.

Still smiling and pretending to talk to each other, the two women began walking toward the southwest corner of the plaza, where two buildings formed a wide corridor. They had only taken a few steps when a shout was heard from behind them, and Nejem turned back to see Darsi raise his submachine gun and begin to fire.

"Get out of here!" She shoved her hostage toward the nearest building, then turned and started going back to help Darsi, only to see two more men with pistols drawn appear from the western side of the plaza. Taking cover behind another planter with a trash receptacle on its other side, they aimed at Darsi and cut loose.

Oh, no you don't, she thought. Ducking behind a nearby planter, Nejem pulled out her cell phone and dialed a number. When it connected, it activated a burner phone wired to one of the improvised explosive devices she and Darsi had created out of the items they had picked up at the store earlier that day.

The powerful homemade bomb near the two men went off in a loud explosion and brief burst of flame. The trash bin seemed to swell for just a moment before bursting apart in a lethal spray of metal fragments. The top flew at least fifty feet into the air before crashing down again into the middle of the plants in the planter next to the destroyed bin, crushing them.

When the smoke cleared, the two men were sprawled a few yards away, both bloody and motionless on the ground. Several bystanders had been caught in the blast as well, but Nejem didn't care about them. Her only thought now was to keep the black-haired man and his companions occupied for as long as possible so Panshin could complete his work.

Pistol in one hand, cell phone in the other, she stayed hunched over as she ran toward the blast site, now the safest place in the plaza. As she approached, Darsi was still firing at people she couldn't see on the other side of him. She would take up this position and watch his back.

As Nejem approached, she saw that one of the gunmen caught in the blast was still alive, although he was badly battered, with trickles of red streaming from his ears and nose. A jagged shard of metal had punched into his upper chest, and his whole shirt was stained with blood. Even though grievously wounded, when he saw her, he tried to raise his pistol, only to see that his hand was empty, the gun having been dropped or blown out of it.

She raised her weapon and put a bullet into his forehead, then hunkered down and watched for anyone else who might be trying to ambush them.

WHEN THE BLAST faded away, Bolan knew only one thing—that the shooters who had been targeting him were no more. He glanced to his left to see Rosnovich and Kepar advancing toward him, weapons drawn, and for a moment he wasn't sure if they were there to kill him or the rogue operatives. He kept his pistol ready in case they were about to try for him, but they just stayed low on their approach and reached the side of the planter next to him, Rosnovich watching the east side, Kepar taking the west.

"The other team—they were yours, weren't they?" Bolan asked.

Rosnovich nodded. "Backup from Paris. We didn't tell you because we weren't sure we could entirely trust you."

Bolan resisted sighing. Cold War habits died hard. "So, can we take out these two out without having to worry about getting a bullet from each other?"

The Russian nodded. "Yes, our common enemy needs to be killed right now. Thoughts?"

"Keep the second shooter's head down while I take out the turbaned one on the other side here."

All during their conversation, the turbaned man had kept firing, indicating he was well equipped.

Rosnovich nodded again, then nudged his partner, quietly speaking several short bursts of Russian.

Meanwhile, Bolan contacted Tokaido. "Where exactly is the second shooter?"

"Just less than ten yards due east of your position. She's at the bomb blast site, providing overwatch for the guy in a turban and making sure no one catches them in a cross fire from behind."

"Got it, thanks."

Bolan turned to look over at the far planter Tokaido

had indicated, and saw a brief flash of movement there. "Okay, Mikhail, keep her head down, and I assume Natalya will distract Turban-head so I can get the drop on him."

"Correct, but how do you plan to do that?"

Bolan nodded at the foliage over their heads. "Straight across. He'll never expect it."

"Gutsy. Good luck." Still crouched, the Russian exchanged places with Bolan, sticking his gun out and sending several shots toward the woman's hiding place. At the same time, Bolan heard Kepar open fire on the other side of him.

Time to move.

Staying as low as he could, the Executioner crawled into the planter, moving aside the various grasses, ferns and flowers instead of crawling over them, so he could still retain some cover. The firing continued on all sides of him now, but no bullets chopped into the plant life around or in front of him, indicating that the others were doing a good job of keeping the two gunners distracted.

The planter was roughly three or four yards across, but it felt twice as wide. Every step had to be carefully planned to disturb as few of the plants around him as possible. One arm at a time, one leg at a time, he got closer and closer to his target.

And then, finally, he carefully pushed aside a thick tuft of grass to catch a glimpse of the turbaned assassin kneeling behind the stone bench as he traded shots with Palomer and Kepar. Slowly, Bolan brought up his pistol, careful not to make any sudden move that might draw the attention of his target. When he had the gun in place, he drew a bead on the man's neck, planning to take him out with one well-placed shot. His finger curled around the trigger—

And the damnable breeze blew again, swaying the tall grasses.

The turbaned man's attention was drawn to the movement, and he and Bolan's gazes locked just as the Executioner squeezed the trigger.

17

The assassin did not drop his weapon and collapse with a fountain of blood spurting between the fingers clutched to his neck.

No, surprisingly he moved out of the path of the bullet the instant before it left the muzzle. He wasn't able to completely dodge the slug—it struck the tip of his chin as he lurched backward, gouging out a chunk of flesh and bone as it passed—but it did not kill him.

What's more, as he was falling, the turbaned shooter was bringing his submachine gun to bear on Bolan, and he fired.

The Executioner hit the dirt as a stream of bullets mowed down the grasses and a small tree just over his head. He stuck his pistol up just far enough to know he could clear the lip of the planter and returned fire blindly, aiming in the general direction of where the shots were coming from and hoping to strike something.

As soon as the shots had started, they stopped, and Bolan realized what that probably meant. Reload!

Rising to his hands and knees, he crawled to the edge

of the planter and, taking a deep breath, raised his pistol up to cover the area behind the bench, ready to fire the moment he saw his target.

The spot was empty, with only a scattering of empty shells and the distinct, fading odor of a fired weapon the only signs he'd been there in the first place. Silence had descended, and Bolan craned his neck to try to see farther into the plaza.

A gun cracked, and a bullet clipped the top of his ear even as a blur of movement from below told him that the assassin was hiding on the ground on the other side of the planter!

Even as he tried to swing his pistol down, a grip as solid as iron grabbed his wrist and pulled hard. Before he could react, Bolan was flipping through the air, landing on the stone bench with breath-stealing force, hard enough to jar his pistol loose from his hand and send it clattering to the ground.

He'd barely hit when he saw the butt of the man's submachine gun blurring down toward his face. Bolan jerked his head out of the way just in time, and the end of the grip smacked hard into the seat next to him. Still trying to draw air into his lungs, he managed to kick up his leg, hitting the top of the man's head hard enough to shove him back a bit.

Bolan rolled off the bench onto the ground and pushed himself back onto his knees just as his attacker tried punting his head off with a front kick. The moment he realized that he'd missed he reversed it faster than any sensei Bolan had ever seen and brought it back down onto his head, hard. The man tried pulling his foot away, but the Executioner grabbed it first and leaned back, intending to pull him off balance, as well.

Instead, the turbaned man rode forward with the

movement and kicked out with his other foot, catching Bolan square in the nose. Fortunately, he was moving back, so the impact wasn't as hard as it could have been, but it still hurt.

Falling onto his butt, Bolan glimpsed the man break his own fall with his hands, so they were both sitting on the ground now. He took the opportunity to kick the submachine gun out of the guy's hand, depriving him of that weapon at least. The only problem was that he seemed just as deadly with his hands and feet.

Bolan still had his adversary's foot trapped, and now he wrenched it as hard as he could to the right, hoping to break or at least sprain the knee or ankle, and gain some sort of advantage. But again the guy rolled with the move like he was a step ahead, turning with it as he kicked at Bolan's fingers with his other boot. The hard sole smashed into his hand, and the assassin did it again, forcing him to let go before any of his fingers were broken.

He didn't have any time to recover or plan an assault, either; the man performed a rising handspring to gain his feet and advanced on Bolan immediately, aiming a punch at his face that would have finished the job his foot had started.

Bolan rolled back to avoid the strike, kicking out with both feet to keep the guy off him, then back-somersaulting onto his feet and going on the offensive himself, lunging forward in an attempt to take his opponent by surprise.

The unorthodox method worked, partially. He did manage to tackle the man, who had been aiming another punch at him, which bounced off his lowered shoulder. Bolan wrapped both arms around him and used his forward momentum to drive him backward off his feet, until both men smashed to the ground.

From cover, her wounded arm throbbing and her gun hand heavy from exchanging fire with the turbaned man, Marie Palomer watched the furiously fighting men go at each other, no quarter asked or given. If she had been 100 percent fit, she would have gone to assist, as hand-to-hand had never phased her. However, with one arm out of commission, she'd be more hindrance than help. Of course, trying to shoot into that close-quarters combat would be even more foolish. She would just have to trust that Cooper could take him down.

Her gaze flicked to the motionless form of the police officer who had almost blown their whole operation. He'd been returning fire along with Palomer, when part of one of the turbaned man's bursts had caught him while he was aiming, taking him down and, by the looks of his wounds, out.

Sirens wailed in the distance, but it would be a few minutes before backup would arrive and lock down the area. Meanwhile, more gunshots sounded on the other side of the plaza, followed by distant screams and shouts, but there was still enough vegetation in the planter in the middle that she couldn't see exactly what was happening over there.

Instead, she noticed a few clusters of people taking cover under the benches or behind the other planters. Stifling a groan, Palomer got to her feet, and staying low, crossed to the nearest group, two women and one man huddled together.

"You need to leave this area immediately," she told them. "There are other bombs here. When I tell you, go quickly and quietly to the street and around the corner of the nearest building." She poked her head up above the planter, but there was no firing—in fact, there didn't seem to be any shooters nearby.

"Okay, go now!" she urged. The women rose first, pulling the obviously terrified man along with them toward the safety of the nearby building. When no shots rang out, Palomer moved to the next group and did the same thing, clearing the entire section.

She scooted over to the next one, which had a trash container next to it, and a family clustered around the corner of the planter. Palomer repeated her message and had gotten the family moving away when she spotted a large white paper bag hidden among the foliage in the planter itself.

Dreading what she would find, she pushed a large fern aside to see the bag begin to vibrate, and she caught the shrill tone of a cell phone ringing inside.

Without even thinking about it, she scrambled up and onto the bag, covering it with her own body to shield anyone still nearby. Squeezing her eyes tightly closed, she heard what sounded like a click and smelled an acrid odor before her entire world erupted in a blinding flash.

As soon as Cooper and the turbaned man began exchanging gunfire, Sevaron and Zimin split up to try to get the drop on the female shooter. He broke left, and she went straight up the middle, gunfire from both of them keeping her head down. A few return shots came from her position, but nothing like the concentrated fire that had been coming from there less than a minute earlier.

Taking cover on the eastern and southern sides of the planter, Sevaron signaled his partner to head around the other side, with him coming at her from the opposite direction in a five-count. It was risky, in that one of them was likely to get shot during the rush forward, but she wouldn't be able to get them both before one put a bullet into her.

At the corner, Sevaron checked his pistol's load while counting to five under his breath, then surged forward, gun out and ready to cut the female shooter down the instant he saw her...

Only she wasn't behind the smoking wreckage of the trash container anymore. He saw Zimin from the corner of his eye, and knew she was covering her side. He also knew she didn't see the woman either, or she'd be shooting.

He did see the lifeless bodies of Sergei Bershov and Illya Krivov on the ground nearby. Sevaron's mouth tightened at the sight, and he scanned the area, looking for any evidence of which way she'd gone.

Screams and shouts, followed by a pair of gunshots farther down the plaza, alerted them to her escape route. Figuring Cooper and Palomer had the other one under control, the two Russians took off into the corridor formed by the two buildings, where several people were huddled against the wall, and two were bent over a woman who had either fallen or been shot to the ground, he wasn't sure which.

"Police, police!" he exclaimed in Spanish as he ran up to them. "Which way did she go?"

The man pointed, and Sevaron said, "Help will be here soon!" as he took off after her.

Feet pounding on the pavement, the two Russians sprinted toward the street at the end of the block. They burst out onto the sidewalk in time to see a blurred figure run up over the roof of a cab, the driver honking its horn angrily. "Come on!" he shouted as he took off after her again.

"Police! Police! Get down! Get down!" he shouted in Spanish as they ran down the crowded sidewalk, both to get people out of their way as well as avoid them getting shot if the assassin suddenly decided to turn and open fire on them. But right now she seemed intent on just trying to put as much distance between her and them as possible.

They chased the shooter for another two blocks, dodging locals and tourists alike, until they came to a construction site where a new skyscraper was going up. The woman cut across traffic in the middle of the street, nearly getting herself run over twice, and setting off a furious fusillade of screeching tires and honking horns.

"Go, go, go!" Sevaron urged, running into the street after her. The cars had just started moving when he appeared, one of them coming so close that its wheel tagged his shoe, almost sending him sprawling. Staggering forward, Sevaron regained his balance and kept moving, clearing the last lane just in time to spot his quarry climbing the security fence ringing the construction site.

"Stop!" he shouted, raising his pistol and firing three rounds at her. But his aim was off from the running, and the bullets punched into the boards around her, one possibly grazing her, but not hitting anything vital. Zimin also fired as she ran up to her partner, but the woman raced to the top of the fence like a monkey and dropped out of sight on the other side.

"After her!" he panted, running to the fence and leaping up to grab the top edge. He was about to pull himself up when a weight tackled him from below, and he lost his grip and fell off. As he did, thunder sounded from the other side of the fence, and several holes appeared in the slats where he had been hanging.

Sevaron hit the sidewalk hard and looked up to see Zimin half on top of him, shaking her head. In his eagerness to catch the assassin, he had almost gotten shot. "Thank you."

"You can thank me when this bitch is dead," she replied. "Now come on!"

They got to their feet and climbed the fence more carefully this time, entering the construction site after their quarry.

18

Carefully drawing a line of epoxy around the edge of the ninth box, Alexei Panshin, aka Samantha George, affixed it in a shadowed corner formed by the end of a row of lights and the side of a support beam running the length of the room.

So far, everything was going exactly as planned. Just as he expected, no one bothered the lighting tech just going around doing "her" job. To keep it real, Panshin had also stopped off at the light board and played with a few programs, checking the status of the system and its controls to ensure that everything was working properly. But the bulk of the past few hours had been spent climbing on the catwalks all around the top of the room, attaching the cubes to the ceiling in precisely calculated places for maximum impact.

By his estimation, he was actually a few minutes ahead of schedule. As he pressed this latest box into place, Panshin wondered how Amani and Kisu were doing. There had been no sign of the dark-haired American or his female partner, nor of the other Russians

anywhere here, so he assumed they had been successful in distracting the others, leaving him to complete
their mission. Even if they had to sacrifice one or both
of their lives, they understood the risks of the job, and
would not hesitate to do so—exactly as they had been
trained to do.

With the box securely in place, Panshin headed back
down the stepladder he had been using to reach the ceiling, and started walking back along the catwalk toward
the main ladder to the floor below.

"Hey, Samantha." Javier Toset stood near the ladder, looking up at Panshin. He nodded at him as he descended, noting the increased activity in the room now.
At least a dozen people milled about, some setting up
name placards in front of chairs, others helping with
last-minute setup of the front area.

"Hi, Javier. Can I help you?"

"Just stopped by to see how things are going. Is there
anything you need to be ready for tomorrow morning?
Any supplies or assistance?"

He looked down at the podium, then up at the lights
that would be illuminating the speakers. "Not at the moment, thank you. Everything is in excellent shape, and
Sara has been a great help to me." He actually hadn't
contacted Sara at all, but in all the rush, it was doubt-
ful the woman would remember who she had or hadn't
talked to during the prep. "Also, my compliments to
your team. They've really done a fantastic job here. In
a couple hours I'll be ready for some lighting checks,
but I can probably just borrow one or two of the staff
members as stand-ins at that time."

"Many of us will be working late into the night, so feel
free to grab anyone who's available when you need them."
Toset's pocket vibrated. He grabbed his phone and glanced

at it with a barely stifled groan. "A manager's job is never done. I have to run. Again, if you need anything, just ask."

"I will, and thank you again, Javier. Together, we're going to make this conference one to remember."

"I certainly hope so," he called over his shoulder as he walked away.

Panshin's smile was absolutely genuine—though not at all for the reasons Toset's was. With a last scan of the area, he turned back to his work.

As HE BORE the other man to the ground, Bolan tried to keep his weight on top so he could incapacitate the guy, but he was like an eel coated in petroleum jelly—slippery as hell.

The second both men hit the ground the assassin bucked up hard, nearly dislodging Bolan, who just barely managed to hang on. Then he threw a knee into Bolan's back, making the area explode with pain. Letting out a grunt, he grabbed for the man's neck with both hands and choked him—or tried to.

The man's windpipe had been reinforced with some sort of highly resistant material that refused to budge under Bolan's hands. Feeling what he was trying to do, the operative actually chuckled at his ineffective efforts. "Weird, isn't it?" he said in unaccented English as he drove his knee hard into Bolan's back again. "Squeeze as much as you want. It will only grow more stiff as you do. But enough of this."

His leg flipped up again, but this time it caught Bolan across the chest and levered him back. That, along with slipping a hand between his forearms and flipping them apart, broke Bolan's hold and sent him flying backward.

The turbaned man did another effortless rising handspring that put him on his feet. "My partner let us know about your encounter with him in the subway," he said as he bounced back and forth on the balls of his feet, hands held loosely at his sides. "I must confess I was looking forward to testing myself against you, but now that you are here, I see he was right—you are obsolete."

Bolan had ended up flat on his back during the assassin's little speech, and now he got up slowly, his lower back feeling like it was on fire. "I wouldn't count me out just yet—"

A nearby blast in a planter rocked the area, shaking them both. The turbaned man glanced over just long enough for Bolan to take advantage, and he stepped forward and swung his foot up with all of his strength, aiming for the one spot on any man that was sure to take even the biggest thug down—right between his legs.

He landed a solid hit to the guy's crotch, feeling the impact all the way up his own leg. His opponent seemed to jackknife over at the attack, but when Bolan tried to extricate his foot, he found it caught firmly between the man's legs.

"The first thing that was modified on us was all vulnerable points," the man said as he drove an elbow into Bolan's knee, making him nearly shout in near-blinding pain as the joint hyperflexed under the impact. "Now during times of stress, the penis and testicles partially retract into the body." Grabbing Bolan's leg, he shoved it up while stepping forward and sweeping his other leg out from under him. He then shoved on Bolan's body, pile-driving him into the ground with a *thud* that cracked two ribs. "That provides almost complete protection for them, rendering an assault like yours meaningless."

Flat on his back for the third time in less than two minutes, Bolan could only wheeze in response. "I very much doubt, however, that you have such built-in protections," his assailant said as he raised his foot and brought it down to crush Bolan's throat. However, the Executioner wasn't there to take it, managing to move aside just enough so that the foot stomped down on the concrete right next to him, leaving the man's knee exposed.

Bolan supposed Utkin may have replaced the cap with a titanium version to increase its striking power, and maybe he'd woven something into the muscles to make them stronger too, but he was pretty sure there wasn't much he could do to improve on the ball and socket joint that already existed—a joint that was very susceptible to off-angle pressure.

He hauled off and fired the heel of his hand at the side of his adversary's knee with every bit of strength he could muster.

The *crack* of the joint breaking was the sweetest sound he'd heard in a long time. The second sweetest was the strangled cry of the man as his leg buckled, and he nearly fell over.

Nearly fell, but didn't.

His face was strained now, however, and red stained his formerly white pant leg where a bone had broken through the skin. However, instead of being incapacitated like Bolan had hoped, the injury just seemed to make him furious.

"You think that will stop me!" he said as he leaped into the air with his good knee aimed down to ram into Bolan's chest. He couldn't hope to block that, but he could redirect the force, lashing a foot up to kick at the leg as hard as he could. The knee shot out toward his head, and the man fell on top of him, still crushing his breath out, but not nearly as devastating as having the knee and 190 pounds of falling man landing on him.

He punched the assassin's head over and over, raining blows on his cheeks, nose and jaw, but none of the shots even phased him.

"Enough. I will end this by finding out how soft your throat is!" Brushing aside Bolan's attacks, the man smoothly pivoted to sit atop him and reached for his throat. Bolan bucked and twisted, but his adversary stayed on him as if glued there. His fingers clamped around the Executioner's windpipe and began to squeeze.

Bolan tried the same hold-breaking move the man had pulled on him, but it didn't work—he just twisted out of it and kept putting on the pressure.

His vision was starting to blur, and in desperation he clawed at the operative's face, catching a corner of his left eye socket and digging in with all his remaining strength. The other man grunted and pulled his face back, but Bolan had long, strong arms and he gouged deeper into the socket, eventually scooping the eye out entirely.

The man growled through gritted teeth and redoubled his efforts. Bolan was only a few seconds from unconsciousness now, and pulled futilely at his iron-rigid fingers. He turned his head away from the grotesque sight of the man's eyeball dangling from the optic nerve on his cheek, and there, less than three feet away, was his pistol on the ground.

As blackness crept in, he scrabbled for it, fingers straining to close around the grips. And then he had it, bringing it up with the last of his strength and squeezing the trigger over and over, feeling something warm and wet spray over his face even as he lost consciousness...

19

Sevaron and Zimin expected bullets to fly at them any second. But that didn't happen; instead, they heard shouts and two gunshots from closer to the half-completed building.

They ran over there, dodging forklifts and trucks hauling materials around the lot. Near a large open space at the front, a group of men in hard hats and yellow vests were clustered around a man lying on the ground. The two Russians crossed to them quickly.

When the men saw the armed pair, they closed ranks around the wounded man, waving them into the building. "We're police," Sevaron said in Spanish. "Did the armed woman go in there?" The men nodded. "Call an ambulance for him." The Russians then headed into the building.

The interior was framed and the floors and walls were up, but it was all bare wallboard and studs. They swept the ground floor, thinking the assassin may have just slipped out the back, but then they heard two shots above their heads.

Running back to the stairs, they began charging up, sweeping and clearing every floor entrance, in case the operative had doubled back and set up an ambush. Five stories up, they met two panicked men and a woman coming down fast. A quick interrogation confirmed that an armed woman was on the eighth floor. Thanking them and sending them down, Sevaron and Zimin continued going up until they reached the eighth floor. Taking positions on either side of the doorway, they cleared the entrance, then proceeded inside.

Plastic sheets had been hung from floor to ceiling to create rough rooms, letting light in, but only allowing partial, blurred vision through them. The wind swept in from the open sides, rustling the sheets and making it hard to hear any other noises.

Dividing the floor into sections, they began clearing a piece at a time. The first part was empty, but as they walked toward the next quadrant, shots rang out, and they dived to the floor, but not fast enough. A trail of fire burned down Sevaron's back as a bullet grazed him, and he felt warm blood begin to flow. The second he hit the floor, he returned fire, bullets slicing through the plastic where the woman had been, but revealing nothing but bare floor and shell casings.

Getting up, they heard footsteps and gave chase. The other side of the building was divided into smaller rooms, and the plastic lining the rough corridors created a kind of maze. Sevaron and Zimin began creeping up and down the crude passageways, their senses alert, straining to get the merest glimpse or catch the faintest noise that would give them an edge.

Movement on his right caught Sevaron's eye, and he glanced at it, starting to bring up his weapon before realizing it was just more flapping plastic. He turned back, only to see a dark shadow moving on his other side, and then the assassin was firing through the plastic at him.

He threw himself back as bullets punched through nearby, one striking his hand. Zimin was there in a second, shooting at the woman even as she ran across the hallway and through another plastic sheet.

Sevaron got to his feet again, holding his hand tight against his body. The bullet had smashed into his middle finger, tearing out a large chunk and rendering his hand useless. He switched his pistol to his other hand.

Seeing his injury, Zimin started to move ahead of him to take the lead, but was stopped by Sevaron's arm. *"Nyet."*

He proceeded ahead of her, pistol at the ready. When they came to the section where the assassin had launched her ambush, he bent and touched his fingers to a splatter of red droplets on the floor. Blood. He rose with a smile. "You hit her."

They began to follow the blood trail. It seemed to be leading back to the stairway, and they quickened their pace, although still trying to move carefully.

Again, the plastic rustled more loudly around them, making it hard to hear. Sevaron had just cleared another room when he turned a corner and saw the operative standing a couple yards down the passageway, aiming her pistol at him. He tried bringing his around, but she squeezed first.

Click. A misfire.

He was still bringing his gun on line when she ran toward him—so fast!—and threw her useless weapon at his head. He ducked out of the way, trying to shoot her at the same time, but she was on him too quickly, and swatted the pistol out of the way as she drove in to attack.

Her first jab was straight at his wounded hand, and

the pain as her fist hit it nearly made him black out. It wasn't that he wasn't used to it—he'd endured his share during training—but the blow was so savage and powerful it broke the bones in his hand.

He fell backward, with her following up the assault with another series of punches and kicks. His retreat, however, brought them both to an entrance into another room—where Zimin lay in wait.

When Sevaron had fallen back far enough, she stepped forward, thrusting her pistol out until it was only an inch from the other woman's head, and squeezed the trigger as fast as she could. Even so, the assassin's incredible reflexes almost allowed her to avoid the bullets.

Almost.

The rounds sparked and careened off her reinforced skull, gouging furrows through her hair and scalp as they carved through flesh and slammed into metal and bone. The curve of her head was enough to deflect most of them, but she still took a good deal of damage from that assault. Even so, she retained enough ability to palm strike Zimin hard enough to shove her back across the room.

By then Sevaron was back up and coming at his adversary. The pressure from the bullets striking her head had done a number on her face, as well. Her nose had taken a round, tearing it away, and another slug had ripped off her upper lip, leaving a smear of blood and exposed gum behind.

He charged her, hammering the butt of his pistol into her face, causing even more blood to spray. She lashed out with a booted foot, but her aim was off, and it impacted his thigh. Even so, it still contained enough power to make him stagger.

Zimin came back at her from the side, charging through the plastic to ram into her. The woman deftly spun to avoid the attack, shoving her along and making her sprawl on the ground.

Sevaron pressed his attack again, but with one hand, he was at a disadvantage, and the operative knew it. He was too slow in pulling back his hand after a strike one time, and that was all it took. She grabbed his wrist and broke it, sending the gun falling to the floor.

Still holding his arm, she took a front kick from Zimin in her wounded side, which actually made her gasp. She blocked the next attack with her other hand, then tried to throw Sevaron into his partner, but got a surprise when he grabbed her with his injured hand, ignoring the flare of agony from it.

Throwing his other arm around her, he drew her to him, squeezing her tight as he picked her off the ground. Her one hand was still free, however, and she rained blows mercilessly on his head and face while he walked forward—straight toward the open side of the building a few yards away.

By the time he got there, his face was a bloody ruin. One ear was torn off, both eyes were swollen shut and his mouth was a jagged ruin of shattered teeth. Even so, he still had the strength to pitch them both off the side of the building, falling almost ninety yards to the ground.

When Zimin reached the bottom, Sevaron was dead, yet the woman was still trying to pull her broken body out of the yard, dragging her twisted legs behind her. The Russian walked around in front of her, kicked the woman onto her back and aimed her weapon at the assassin's battered, swollen face.

"I just wanted this to be the last thing you saw before

you died," she said before pulling the trigger and emptying the magazine into the assassin's head.

That stopped her from moving—permanently.

20

"Senor? Senor?"

"Agent Cooper? Agent Cooper, can you hear me?"

For the second time in as many days, Bolan regained consciousness to find people hovering over him. The Russian agent, Natalya Kepar, was there, as well as two armed and armored special weapons officers, and a pair of paramedics. Upon seeing him react to their words, the group of people visibly relaxed.

Bolan blinked, then swallowed, grimacing as his injured throat rebelled against the stimulus. Feeling dampness on his face, he wiped his forehead and brought his hand down to see red-brown spots smeared on it. Looking down, he saw that his chest was also spattered with drying blood.

He made a drinking motion with his hand, and a bottle of cold water was pressed into his palm. Bolan drank half of it, ignoring the smaller wave of pain accompanying each swallow, then handed it back to one of the medical personnel with a grateful nod.

He pushed himself up to a sitting position, tensing as

flares of pain radiated across his body. Looking around, he saw a sheet-covered body three feet or so away, and pointed.

"Is that him?" he croaked.

One of the tactical units pulled back the sheet to reveal the face of the turbaned man, now slack in death. "Looked like you emptied your entire magazine into him."

Bolan looked down to see his pistol lying next to him, the slide locked back. "That's because I did." He looked back up at Kepar, who looked as bad as he felt, with bruises on her face and one arm in a sling. "What about his partner?"

"Dead," she replied.

"And Mikhail?"

She shook her head. "He's gone, along with our backup. I'm the only one left of our team."

"I'm sorry to hear that," Bolan said, and he was sincere. Despite what mission they shared or didn't, it was never a good thing to lose personnel on an op, especially in a close-knit team. Then, realizing who else was missing, he looked around again. "Where's Sergeant Palomer?"

"She's gone, too, Striker," Akira Tokaido said in his ear. "While evacuating civilians from the plaza, she found another one of the bombs, which was apparently about to detonate. She covered it with her body just before it exploded."

That hit Bolan hard. He'd only known her for the past two days, but Marie Palomer had been a first-rate field agent, who took her duty seriously, and who he'd enjoyed working with. From what he could tell, she had died just like she had lived—doing her duty, with no thought to the personal cost or sacrifice.

"Inform the DGSI, but have them keep it private for now," Bolan ordered Tokaido as he got to his feet and looked around. "Then tell me you have something on the third operative."

"I think so, yes. We've been running facial recognition on everyone at the convention center since early this morning. We have a match confirmed at 93 percent in the same room the President is supposed to be speaking in tomorrow morning."

"All right, thanks."

Bolan looked Kepar in the eyes. "We've got a match back at the convention center. I'm heading there now to finish this. I'd imagine that you want to be there, too."

She nodded, her face stony. "I wouldn't miss it for anything."

"Now, who's in charge here?" Bolan asked everyone as he looked around.

"I am, senor." A lean tactical-operations man with a salt-and-pepper goatee stepped forward. "Lieutenant Alfonse Macado. How can I help you?"

"Once you're sure that the area is secure, I want you to give a very specific press conference, and this is what I want you to say…"

A SMALL, SATISFIED GRIN on his face, Alexei Panshin finished securing the last ceramic cube to the ceiling of the auditorium.

He climbed down the stepladder and folded it, carrying it with him as he headed back toward the main ladder. On the way, he wondered what had happened to Amani and Kisu. They hadn't contacted him in more than an hour, which might have been due to one of several things, but most likely meant they had been intercepted or killed while executing their mission. It would be a shame if that had happened, but again, they would have given their lives in the service of their country, and that was all that mattered.

As he started heading down the ladder, the public address system crackled to life: "May I have your attention, please. We have just been informed that there has been an incident in the AZCA financial district of Madrid this afternoon. At least two persons planted and detonated explosive devices in a public plaza and opened fire on bystanders. Several people were injured, and at least three were killed before the gunmen were killed. The police have assured us that the area has been secured, and that there is no more danger. At this time, we are continuing to move forward with the summit as originally planned. Everyone is to continue their work as previously directed. Please see your section leaders if you have any questions. Thank you for your attention and cooperation." The announcement was made in several languages.

That pretty much clinched it—his teammates had fallen. Panshin could only hope they had eliminated as many of the people chasing them as possible. If he was lucky, they might think he was among the dead now, allowing him to make his escape unnoticed. But regardless of whether he lived or died, nothing could stop the carnage he had planned for this day.

With the stepladder over his shoulder, he started down the left aisle toward the rear doors, intending to get to the truck and get out of the area. The normal buzz of people working throughout the room had lessened somewhat, but that made sense, as this space was just about ready.

Panshin reached the main floor, and was about to pass the last audience table when the black-haired man, looking like he had just been in a vicious fight, stepped through the left lower door only a few yards away, a black submachine gun snugged tight to his shoulder and aimed directly at Panshin's heart.

"OKAY, WE'RE SURE that's the operative?" From outside the room, Bolan watched on his phone as a redheaded woman came down the ladder, carrying a small step-ladder. She stopped as the announcement about the incident in the city was broadcast over the loudspeaker. The main assassin in Paris was a male, and as Bolan knew these people were masters of disguise.

"Affirmative, Striker," Tokaido replied. "She's been busy setting up some sort of series of black boxes on the ceiling. They're supposed to be part of the lighting system, but could contain explosives, or a toxic gas dispersal system, or who knows what. The point is, that's your guy, er, gal."

"Right." Bolan glanced at Genoveva Prieto. "Is everyone in position?" They'd been watching the operative work for the past several minutes while pulling everyone out of the room one and two at a time and replacing them with undercover security personnel carrying hidden weapons. Now except for her, everyone else working in the auditorium was from the center's security.

"Yes, although I still wish you would let my people handle this—" she began.

"Thank you, but with the US President scheduled to appear here in less than twelve hours, I've assumed command," Bolan said. "Feel free to lodge a complaint with your higher-ups. They'll find that I have the authority."

While he thought her people would probably do a good job, Bolan was going to finish this himself. He had to be sure it was over.

Their target started walking down the aisle toward the speaker's podium. "All security personnel are to go only on my mark," Bolan said to Prieto, who nodded and spoke rapidly into her radio.

He looked at Kepar, who was standing behind him, pistol in hand. "Ready?"

She nodded. "Ready."

He pushed the door open and led with an HK MP5A braced tightly against his shoulder, aiming straight at the "woman," who stopped and stared in shock at him. "What do you think you're doing—"

"I'm arresting you on the charges of murder, attempted murder, terrorism and a whole lot of other crimes I'm sure we can hang on you before we're through," Bolan rasped as Kepar stepped up to his side, her own weapon also pointed at the woman. "Keep your hands where I can see them. Any sudden moves will be responded to with deadly force."

Panshin calmly looked around, only to see the same thing in every direction—hard-faced men and women blocking every exit, all pointing pistols at him. Slowly, he began raising his hands…

A jumpsuited young man with long hair pulled himself out from under a cloth-covered table, earbuds blasting music, and began to get to his feet.

"No!" Kepar cried, but it was too late. Panshin struck like a pouncing panther, grabbing the totally unaware man around the neck and slipping behind him. In a moment, a small black pistol was aimed at his head as Panshin yanked the earbuds out of his ears.

"Stop right there and let him go," Bolan ordered.

"Here's what is going to happen now," Panshin said. "You are going to clear the people from the back exit, and I am going to take my hostage out to my truck. We will be allowed to drive off the grounds without challenge and without being followed. I will drive three miles away, and then I will let the young man go. If I spot any tricks, or see anyone trying to follow us, the man will die first. Are we clear?"

"I can't let you leave—"

"What you think you can or cannot do does not matter," Panshin replied. "All that matters is allowing us to walk out of this building right now. If you comply with my directives, he will be released unharmed. If you do not, he will be the next one to die. It is that simple. I am going to start walking to the rear door now. If anyone tries to stop me, this man's death will be on your conscience."

Panshin began heading toward the front of the room, with Bolan tracking him every step of the way. He was good, using the guy's bulk to shield his body, with only about half of his face visible at one time. The distance between them was less than ten yards, but even if Bolan got a shot he could take, there was no guarantee that he would put him down with one bullet. All it would take was an errant muscle twitch or death spasm, and the young man's brains would be sprayed all over the wall.

He had almost reached the exit door by now, the two men nearer to it giving way to the operative. It would be now or never—if he let him get through the door, they'd have even less chance of stopping him.

Bolan took a deep breath and let it out, pushing all of his pain and exhaustion aside. There was only the target now in his vision, a small spot, less than an inch wide, the crosshairs of his scope firmly centered on it. As his target reached for the door handle, Bolan exhaled, and in the space between heartbeats, squeezed the trigger.

The 3-round burst of armor-piercing bullets entered

the assassin's head exactly where Bolan had aimed, through the left eye. Although the cavity was reinforced, the thin titanium shield couldn't withstand the hardened steel penetrator core of the bullets, and let them all in to plow through the brain.

It was like hitting a light switch. Before the echoes of the report died away, Panshin fell to the floor, the unfired pistol sliding from his hand. The terrified worker stumbled away from the twitching body as other security personnel rushed over.

Bolan lowered his weapon with a weary sigh and handed it to one of the center's security personnel.

"It's over," Kepar said from beside him. "Thank you for allowing me to be here. Someone else might not have been so understanding."

Bolan nodded. "No, I get it. You'll let your people know they've been stopped, right?"

"Of course. In fact, there is no need for me to remain here anymore." With a nod at him, she turned and slipped out through the approaching throng.

"All right, Genoveva, you'll probably want to clear the room and get the bomb squad in here to check out whatever she did to the ceiling," Bolan said, stepping aside as people continued to stream into the room. "Time for me to go, too."

Epilogue

One month later

At 0125, Mack Bolan stood in the cargo bay of a C-130J Super Hercules that was traveling at more than 400 miles per hour at an altitude of sixty-five thousand feet off the coast of Russia.

Siberia, to be more precise.

The red light that indicated they were approaching the drop zone flashed twice, and he got to his feet and watched the ramp lower, letting in the freezing air and near-gale force wind. Bolan made one last check to ensure that his face mask and oxygen tank were working.

The light switched from red to green. He trotted forward and launched himself into the night.

Assuming the classic parachutist's free-fall position—arms spread out and bent at right angles to his body, legs spread and bent at the knees—he fell like a rock. The noise of the plane faded quickly, and Bolan was left with only the air rushing past his body and his thoughts as he rapidly approached the ground.

The past thirty days had been busy. The boxes placed by "Samantha George" had all been recovered and neutralized, and the EU summit had gone off without a hitch. The President had delivered a rousing speech lauding the steps the Union had taken so far, and pledging America's staunch support on all future matters, from economic guidance to standing with the Union against all enemies. During his recovery, Bolan had attended Sergeant Marie Palomer's funeral in Paris, where she was buried with full honors, with the press naming her "the hero of Madrid" for her selfless sacrifice. From there, it was back to the States, where there was just one last item to check off—the current location of Dr. Utkin. Kurtzman and Tokaido had searched for him in their off-hours between other missions, and had located where they thought he was after weeks of tracking potential routes and scouring the Siberian tundra, examining high-resolution satellite passes over thousands of square miles.

And now, after figuring out the best way to extract him, Bolan was plummeting down to the frigid landscape in hopes of taking the doctor alive and bringing him to the States so the Department of Defense could tap into his knowledge. Utkin was a genius in his field, there was no doubt, and the United States wanted that information.

A tone chirped in Bolan's helmet, indicating he'd reached the altitude for optimum parachute release. Bolan pulled his rip cord, and the chute billowed free and unfurled overhead, slowing him with a jerk, and slowing his approach to the barren, inhospitable-looking ground below.

With less than fifteen hundred feet to go, he reached the snowy surface in less than a minute, flaring the chute to slow him enough to land on his feet. Bolan hit the quick-release system and grabbed the chute before it could billow away, hiding it and his high-altitude-jump equipment a near a cluster of rocks.

There was only a light dusting of snow around here, as winter hadn't set in yet, and once he got his bearings, he set out in the direction of his target, about three-quarters of a mile away. His insulated suit kept him comfortable, if not toasty in the -20 degrees Celsius night. He was grateful there was no wind.

Although Bolan kept a sharp eye out, Kurtzman and Tokaido were also watching his back from high overhead. After thirty minutes of steady walking, Bolan crested a small rise, only to stare in surprise at the scene before him.

Where there should have been a small, snug mountain cabin now stood only a smoldering pile of ashes and charred timbers, with just the stone chimney still standing. Bolan swept left, then right, in case a welcoming party had been lying in wait for him, then walked down to the ruins, contacting Kurtzman on the way.

"Stony Base, this is Striker, are you getting this through my feed?"

"Striker, this is Stony Base, we're seeing it. The sat feed still shows the cabin as standing, however. Can you verify your coordinates, over?"

"Bear, please," Bolan replied. "You know exactly where I'm standing, don't you?"

"Yeah, yeah, a guy can hope, right? You know what this means, right?"

"Yeah, we just got played," Bolan said as he began poking through the still-warm remains of the building to verify that there was no body there.

"Not just played. They were able to broadcast an alternate signal for our satellites to pick up," Kurtzman said. "Anyone able to do that is connected high up in the surveillance grid, which could mean more trouble down the road in other hot spots."

"The place is empty. Site's still warm, however, which means they were probably here within the past twelve hours. Assuming Utkin was even here in the first place, someone—the Russians or someone else—got to him first."

"Great. Well, come on home, and we'll pick up the search again bright and early tomorrow morning. Stony Base out."

"Affirmative, Striker out," Bolan said, then got on the horn to call the C-130J back to pick up him. Climbing to the top of the tallest hill in the area, which wasn't saying much, he activated a small pack on his back, sending a large, bright yellow balloon a hundred yards into the air.

Soon he heard the roar of propellers as the Super Hercules swooped out of the night sky. A V-shaped catcher at the front of the plane caught the cable and held it, jerking Bolan into the air and trailing him after the airplane. Crew members brought him back on board, and soon Bolan was back in the hold of the aircraft, gratefully accepting a hot cup of coffee.

But all during the flight back, one thought kept nagging at him: Who had Utkin, and where was he now?

Eight hours later
Undisclosed location

HANDS CUFFED BEHIND his back, a hood covering his head, Dr. Rostislav Utkin was marched down a damp hallway and into a small room, where he was forced into a chair. His restraints were removed, but the hood stayed, and his captors left, closing what sounded like a heavy metal door behind them.

Utkin sat up straight, facing his unknown future without fear. No matter what they did to him now, he knew his program was effective. He knew the operatives he had created were effective. Only the interference of the damnable Americans had foiled his plan. Normally, he would try again, but considering how he had been kidnapped from his remote location and spirited away to—wherever he was now, all he expected was interrogation, perhaps torture, followed by death.

Instead, a familiar voice said, "You may remove the hood, Dr. Utkin."

Utkin pulled it off, blinking in the light. As his eyes adjusted, they widened in surprise to see the man standing in front of him—the last person he expected to see.

"I am sure that you have many questions," Colonel General Oleg Istrakov said. "And we will answer as many as we can in time. But first—" he strode forward and stretched out his hand "—let me be the first to congratulate you."

Numbly, Utkin took his hand, and Istrakov shook it vigorously. "I—I don't understand…"

"All will be made clear in time. For now, suffice it to say that you are among friends, Doctor," Istrakov said. "It takes great courage to act according to your beliefs, even when your superiors and your country tells you no. With the activation of your people, you passed the test, showing that you were willing to go against everything you had been told to do what you thought was right. That bold action will pay many dividends, starting right now."

Hope crept into the doctor's voice. "You mean…my program is reactivated?"

"More than back on, my good doctor," Istrakhov

said with a smile. "It's being accelerated. The proof of what your operatives did was everything we hoped for, thereby confirming that your work should—no, *must*—continue."

"Thank you, I look forward to resuming it…" Utkin trailed off as a thought struck him. "But if I may ask, who is this 'we' you referred to a moment ago?"

"Like you, Doctor, there is a group of, shall we say, like-minded individuals in the Russian government who feel the motherland's plans are progressing slower than we would like. Through judicious allocation of funds, equipment and personnel, we are creating our own network of people and units to accelerate the reemergence of the Soviet state, and our ascent to the most powerful nation on the planet again. Your created soldiers are an important part of that plan, Doctor."

Istrakov stood in front of Utkin. "I know that you feel the same way about our homeland, Doctor." He held out his hand. "Will you help us reclaim her lost glory?"

Tears swam in the doctor's eyes as he grasped the man's hand. "With all my heart, yes."

Istrakov pulled him to his feet. "Then come, we have much work to do. And you have to review the status of your other subjects."

"You mean they are still intact and together?" Utkin asked.

"Of course. As the vanguard of our new army, we needed to keep them safe, yes?"

Istrakov threw his arm around the physician as they left the room. "You and I are going to do great things in the coming years, Doctor. Great things."

* * * * *

REQUEST YOUR FREE BOOKS!
2 FREE NOVELS PLUS 2 FREE GIFTS!

HHARLEQUIN®

INTRIGUE

BREATHTAKING ROMANTIC SUSPENSE

YES! Please send me 2 FREE Harlequin® Intrigue novels and my 2 FREE gifts (gifts are worth about $10). After receiving them, if I don't wish to receive any more books, I can return the shipping statement marked "cancel." If I don't cancel, I will receive 6 brand-new novels every month and be billed just $4.74 per book in the U.S. or $5.49 per book in Canada. That's a savings of at least 12% off the cover price! It's quite a bargain! Shipping and handling is just 50¢ per book in the U.S. and 75¢ per book in Canada.* I understand that accepting the 2 free books and gifts places me under no obligation to buy anything. I can always return a shipment and cancel at any time. Even if I never buy another book, the two free books and gifts are mine to keep forever.

182/382 HDN GH3D

Name   (PLEASE PRINT)

Address   Apt. #

City   State/Prov.   Zip/Postal Code

Signature (if under 18, a parent or guardian must sign)

Mail to the **Reader Service:**
IN U.S.A.: P.O. Box 1867, Buffalo, NY 14240-1867
IN CANADA: P.O. Box 609, Fort Erie, Ontario L2A 5X3

**Are you a subscriber to Harlequin® Intrigue books
and want to receive the larger-print edition?
Call 1-800-873-8635 or visit www.ReaderService.com.**

* Terms and prices subject to change without notice. Prices do not include applicable taxes. Sales tax applicable in N.Y. Canadian residents will be charged applicable taxes. Offer not valid in Quebec. This offer is limited to one order per household. Not valid for current subscribers to Harlequin Intrigue books. All orders subject to credit approval. Credit or debit balances in a customer's account(s) may be offset by any other outstanding balance owed by or to the customer. Please allow 4 to 6 weeks for delivery. Offer available while quantities last.

Your Privacy—The Reader Service is committed to protecting your privacy. Our Privacy Policy is available online at www.ReaderService.com or upon request from the Reader Service.

We make a portion of our mailing list available to reputable third parties that offer products we believe may interest you. If you prefer that we not exchange your name with third parties, or if you wish to clarify or modify your communication preferences, please visit us at www.ReaderService.com/consumerchoice or write to us at Reader Service Preference Service, P.O. Box 9062, Buffalo, NY 14240-9062. Include your complete name and address.

HII5

REQUEST YOUR FREE BOOKS!
2 FREE NOVELS PLUS 2 FREE GIFTS!

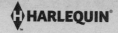

ROMANTIC suspense

Sparked by danger, fueled by passion

YES! Please send me 2 FREE Harlequin® Romantic Suspense novels and my 2 FREE gifts (gifts are worth about $10). After receiving them, if I don't wish to receive any more books, I can return the shipping statement marked "cancel." If I don't cancel, I will receive 4 brand-new novels every month and be billed just $4.74 per book in the U.S. or $5.49 per book in Canada. That's a savings of at least 12% off the cover price! It's quite a bargain! Shipping and handling is just 50¢ per book in the U.S. and 75¢ per book in Canada.* I understand that accepting the 2 free books and gifts places me under no obligation to buy anything. I can always return a shipment and cancel at any time. Even if I never buy another book, the two free books and gifts are mine to keep forever.

240/340 HDN GH3P

Name	(PLEASE PRINT)

Address		Apt. #

City	State/Prov.	Zip/Postal Code

Signature (if under 18, a parent or guardian must sign)

Mail to the **Reader Service:**
IN U.S.A.: P.O. Box 1867, Buffalo, NY 14240-1867
IN CANADA: P.O. Box 609, Fort Erie, Ontario L2A 5X3

Want to try two free books from another line?
Call 1-800-873-8635 or visit www.ReaderService.com.

* Terms and prices subject to change without notice. Prices do not include applicable taxes. Sales tax applicable in N.Y. Canadian residents will be charged applicable taxes. Offer not valid in Quebec. This offer is limited to one order per household. Not valid for current subscribers to Harlequin Romantic Suspense books. All orders subject to credit approval. Credit or debit balances in a customer's account(s) may be offset by any other outstanding balance owed by or to the customer. Please allow 4 to 6 weeks for delivery. Offer available while quantities last.

Your Privacy—The Reader Service is committed to protecting your privacy. Our Privacy Policy is available online at www.ReaderService.com or upon request from the Reader Service.

We make a portion of our mailing list available to reputable third parties that offer products we believe may interest you. If you prefer that we not exchange your name with third parties, or if you wish to clarify or modify your communication preferences, please visit us at www.ReaderService.com/consumerchoice or write to us at Reader Service Preference Service, P.O. Box 9062, Buffalo, NY 14240-9062. Include your complete name and address.

WESTERN WP PROMISES

YES! Please send me **The Western Promises Collection** in Larger Print. This collection begins with 3 FREE books and 2 FREE gifts (gifts valued at approx. $14.00 retail) in the first shipment, along with the other first 4 books from the collection! If I do not cancel, I will receive 8 monthly shipments until I have the entire 51-book Western Promises collection. I will receive 2 or 3 FREE books in each shipment and I will pay just $4.99 US/ $5.89 CDN for each of the other four books in each shipment, plus $2.99 for shipping and handling per shipment. *If I decide to keep the entire collection, I'll have paid for only 32 books, because 19 books are FREE! I understand that accepting the 3 free books and gifts places me under no obligation to buy anything. I can always return a shipment and cancel at any time. My free books and gifts are mine to keep no matter what I decide.

272 HCN 3070 472 HCN 3070

Name	(PLEASE PRINT)

Address	Apt. #

City	State/Prov.	Zip/Postal Code

Signature (if under 18, a parent or guardian must sign)

Mail to the **Reader Service:**

IN U.S.A.: P.O. Box 1867, Buffalo, NY 14240-1867
IN CANADA: P.O. Box 609, Fort Erie, Ontario L2A 5X3

* Terms and prices subject to change without notice. Prices do not include applicable taxes. Sales tax applicable in N.Y. Canadian residents will be charged applicable taxes. This offer is limited to one order per household. All orders subject to approval. Credit or debit balances in a customer's account(s) may be offset by any other outstanding balance owed by or to the customer. Please allow 4 to 6 weeks for delivery. Offer available while quantities last. Offer not available to Quebec residents.

READERSERVICE.COM

Manage your account online!

- Review your order history
- Manage your payments
- Update your address

We've designed the Reader Service website just for you.

Enjoy all the features!

- Discover new series available to you, and read excerpts from any series.
- Respond to mailings and special monthly offers.
- Connect with favorite authors at the blog.
- Browse the Bonus Bucks catalog and online-only exculsives.
- Share your feedback.

Visit us at:

ReaderService.com